Fallen Angel

A Cross Security Investigation

G.K. Parks

Copyright © 2020 G.K. Parks

A Modus Operandi imprint

All rights reserved.

ISBN:
ISBN-13: 978-1-942710-20-2

For my mom and dad

BOOKS IN THE LIV DEMARCO SERIES:

Dangerous Stakes
Operation Stakeout
Unforeseen Danger
Deadly Dealings

BOOKS IN THE ALEXIS PARKER SERIES:

Outcomes and Perspective
Likely Suspects
The Warhol Incident
Mimicry of Banshees
Suspicion of Murder
Racing Through Darkness
Camels and Corpses
Lack of Jurisdiction
Dying for a Fix
Intended Target
Muffled Echoes
Crisis of Conscience
Misplaced Trust
Whitewashed Lies
On Tilt
Purview of Flashbulbs
The Long Game
Burning Embers
Thick Fog

BOOKS IN THE JULIAN MERCER SERIES:

Condemned
Betrayal
Subversion
Reparation
Retaliation

ONE

"Don't be shy." I gave the red-headed woman at the door my most engaging smile. "I won't bite."

"No, I um..." she looked uncertainly at my secretary, "I made a mistake. I got the wrong office."

The black stenciling on the frosted glass was impossible to mistake. *Cross Security and Investigations.* I thought I was clever using the initials CSI. So far, no one else seemed to think so, but it'd catch on, unless Jerry Bruckheimer sued me. Then it would really catch on.

"Are you sure?" The dark bruises on her upper arm and the poorly executed attempt to cover her split lip and black eye didn't go by unnoticed.

"Yeah, sorry to bother you." She hesitated, like a deer caught in headlights, frozen and unsure if she should run.

I stood and grabbed my jacket, slipping it on over my crisp white shirt. A remnant of my brief stint working on Wall Street. "No bother at all." She didn't need charming. She needed a friend. Someone she could trust. "I was just about to grab some coffee." I shook off my receptionist's questioning look. The last thing I needed was for her to mention the espresso machine in the back room. "Can I help you find the right office?"

"No." The redhead stumbled backward, afraid.

I tried the smile again, more subdued and less engaging this time. I didn't want to frighten her more than she already was. "How about you let me buy you a cup of coffee instead?"

She shook her head.

I should have given up. Obviously, she changed her mind. If she didn't want my help, I couldn't force it on her. Domestic issues were sticky, but her bruises made my blood boil.

"Suit yourself." I turned to my assistant. "Have our calls forwarded to the service. Since this lovely young lady doesn't need our help, I say we cut out early tonight."

"Are there any special messages you want relayed if the commissioner calls?"

There were plenty of things I wanted to say to that bastard, but none of them were polite to repeat in front of mixed company. "No."

"Very good, sir." Justin picked up the phone and pressed a few keys.

The woman lingered just outside the doorway. I glanced at her from the corner of my eye as I stepped into the corridor. "Are you sure there isn't something I can do for you?" But the question only agitated her more. I cleared my throat. "How rude of me. I haven't even introduced myself. I'm Lucien Cross."

"Jade McNamara," she said out of habit.

"Nice to meet you." I pushed the button for the elevator. "Are you sure I can't buy you a cup of coffee?"

"I don't know. Maybe."

I nodded and politely gestured at the open elevator doors. She stepped inside, tucking herself into the rear corner. I stepped in and pressed the button for the lobby, keeping as much distance between us as possible in the hopes it would make her more comfortable.

"Were you looking for King Realtors?"

"No." Her eyebrows pinched together. "Why would you think that?"

"I bought my office space from them." I shook my head, realizing I wasn't making much sense. "They used to occupy the space I'm in now. Come to think of it, they also sold me the property."

"Oh. Good for you." She picked at the peeling polish on her thumbnail. "Do you get a commission for recommending them?"

I laughed. "No." I turned my head, watching as she continued to stare at her nails and the floor. "But since you weren't looking for me, I thought maybe you were looking for them."

She didn't say anything.

I only hung my shingle a few weeks ago. This security and investigation thing was new to me. Sure, I had business savvy and plenty of thoughts and ideas on how to make it work. I planned to specialize in corporate clients. My business background and trader status had led to a lot of contacts. I already had a list of clients lined up who needed employee background checks, security details for CEOs, and advice on internet protections. I was set. Cross Security would take off soon enough. I didn't actually need to investigate anything. But I wanted to as a matter of pride.

Until now, I never had a walk-in. If I were smart, I'd let her walk away. This wasn't my area of expertise. But it could be. I was nothing if not a go-getter.

"Did you file a police report?"

Her gaze shot up, the panic evident with the clenching of her jaw and barely contained tremor. "I don't know what you're talking about."

"The bruises around your eye and that split lip say otherwise."

"I fell."

"Is that how you got marks on your arm made by someone's fingers? He was just helping you up, right?"

She tugged on her sleeve, wishing she wore long sleeves instead. "How did you even see that?"

"I notice things. That's why it's Cross Security and Investigations." My private investigator license application was pending, but she didn't need to know that. Idly, I wondered about the legal ramifications of taking a case without being licensed. I'd have to call my attorney in the morning, but since I fulfilled the requirements, including the apprenticeship and training, I didn't think it would matter. I'd be approved. There was no doubt about it.

The elevator doors opened. "I should go." She beelined out of the car.

"Ms. McNamara, wait. I didn't mean to upset you. Please, let me buy you a cup of coffee."

She spun, halfway between the elevator and the front door. "I don't need your help."

I stared into her eyes. "You need someone's help. That's why you came to my office today. Let's talk about it."

She turned back around, intent on getting as far away from me as possible.

"There's a shelter on Eighth. If you won't let me help you, at least let them help you."

She stopped in her tracks. Building security and a few businesspeople stared at us. This wasn't a good way to conduct myself in public. I should have stayed in my office.

"I can't go there," she said, facing away from me. "He'll find me."

TWO

"Are you sure you don't want a cookie?"

Jade had been eyeing the giant rainbow chip cookies since the moment we stepped into the café. She shook her head, reaching for her cup which rattled against the saucer as she lifted it. Getting her to agree to coffee had been like pulling teeth, so convincing her to eat a cookie or a sandwich was out of the question. I slipped the barista a couple of twenties with the understanding that she'd check on us periodically and refill our mugs. Leaving Jade unattended would cause her to bolt, and I didn't want that to happen until I heard her story.

"Isn't this lovely weather we're having?" I hoped to get her talking. She had shut down as soon as we stepped foot inside the coffee shop.

She stared at me over the rim of her mug. "Sure, I guess."

I ran a hand through my hair, realizing I'd done it a dozen times in the last ten minutes. "Do you think I should shave my head?"

"What?" she sputtered.

I shrugged. "I obviously have a nervous tic. Maybe it would alleviate the problem, but I might turn into one of those guys who rubs his head all the time. I could always just carry a towel and polish my head like a bowling ball."

Her eyes lit up, and her lips quirked in the corners. Either she thought I was insane, or she was amused. "What the hell's wrong with you?"

"Plenty."

She sobered. "Me too."

"Do you want to tell me about it? About him?"

She looked around the room, making sure no one was within earshot or paying any attention to us. "I moved here for graduate school. Criminal justice, of all things." She snorted. "Isn't that fucking ironic?" She fell silent, so I waited her out.

Finally, I gestured to the barista and asked for a cookie. Even if Jade didn't want one, I needed something to do to pass the time. Patience wasn't my strong suit. I wanted things done now. Maybe that was the downside of spending two years on the trading floor. But I suspected that flaw wasn't because of my previous profession; it was just who I was. And I had grown accustomed to getting what I wanted when I wanted it.

I broke the cookie in half and took a bite. "How long ago was that?"

"Five years." She eyed the remaining piece of cookie, so I pushed the plate closer to her. "That's how I met him. At first, things were great. He was great. Attentive and funny, everything a girl could ever want and more. But something happened, and he changed. The first time," she bit her lip and stared at the espresso maker, "he said he was sorry. He promised it wouldn't happen again. And for the next four months, it didn't."

"That's what they all say," I mumbled. "How long have you two been together?"

"Three and a half years. I met him while researching my thesis. He let me do a ride along." She blinked, taking a deep breath.

"He's a cop?"

"A sergeant."

"The police department takes allegations of domestic abuse seriously. Have you filed a complaint?"

"No."

"That's the first thing you should do." I wiped my hands on a napkin and reached for my phone. "Have you called 9-1-1 for help?"

"No."

I tried to recall everything I'd been taught. "What about doctor's visits or trips to the ER? Did you have any of these injuries documented?"

"No. I don't have insurance, and it's never been that bad."

I stared at her. "No, Ms. McNamara, it is bad. You know that. That's why you sought help. Have you tried breaking up with him?"

"Once." Her eyes grew bright and wet. "I shouldn't be talking to you. I shouldn't be here."

"What did he do when you left him?"

She swallowed and stared at the cookie crumbs on the plate. "He found me. He'll always find me. He doesn't want me to leave. Going would be suicide. I know it."

"Have you considered filing a restraining order?"

"How can I? We live together."

"Still?" I didn't understand, but no one could unless they were in that position.

A fire ignited inside of her. "You don't get it. We've been together for a long time. He is my everything. I barely scrape by. I work in a place just like this. I can't afford rent or utilities. I don't have any family here. The friends I had are gone now. I have nowhere else to go, and even if I did, I wouldn't survive without him."

"He chipped away at your other connections." I didn't need her to answer. I knew enough to know this is how situations like this started. The abuser craved a sense of power and control over the abused, even though the reason for his behavior was often because of his own fear and insecurities. He wanted her alone and all to himself. He needed to be needed, so he created the ideal situation to make that happen. Honestly, I didn't give a shit about the psychology. I just wanted to break the cycle and this guy's face. "There are resources available to you." I scrolled through my contacts, jotting down names and numbers as

I went.

"He's a cop. There's no place I can go where he can't find me."

"I disagree, but we aren't there yet." I watched her nibble on the end of the cookie. "Before this goes any further, I need to ask you something."

"What?"

"Are you prepared to leave him for good?"

"I don't see how I can."

"Don't worry about the logistics. I just need to know if you're done with him. You came to my office, but I get the sense you might not be ready. Until you are, there's nothing anyone can do to help you." It was the hard truth. I wouldn't lie or sugarcoat things. She had to commit to this. If she couldn't, there was no point, and I didn't have the time or resources to waste if she intended to run back to him in a few days or weeks. "Do you still love him?"

"No. I haven't for a long time. Honestly, I think I hate him. Last night, he came home drunk. Angry and," she took an unsteady breath, tears welling in her eyes, though she wouldn't let them fall, "looking for a fight. I said something stupid about not wanting to put up with his shit anymore, and that set him off. He," she fought to hold back the emotions, "pulled his gun on me and said he'd kill me if I ever leave him."

THREE

I had to be smart about this. Every cell in my body wanted to march into the police station and beat the shit out of Sergeant Scott Renwin, but a frontal assault would only lead to more problems. And I was in the business of solving problems, not creating them.

A framed photo stood on the mantle, and I picked it up. The two of them were at the beach. Jade was laughing as a wave crashed down around them. She was beautiful, with alabaster skin, fiery red hair, and sharp teal eyes. Renwin wasn't anything special, which I should have realized in the coffee shop when she said what initially drew her to him was his sense of humor. That spoke volumes for his looks. What did a woman like her ever see in a guy like him?

"He'll know I left," Jade tossed another item into her duffel bag, "especially after our fight last night. As soon as he gets home, he'll start looking for me. How long do you think it'll take him to find me when he has the entire police department at his disposal? A few hours, maybe?"

"That's why you're leaving a note saying your aunt unexpectedly took ill and you had to go to her. Once we get your things packed and clear out, you should call him and tell him about your unexpected trip."

"You want me to talk to him?"

"You don't have to. We'll do whatever you think is best."
I reread the brief message she had written and hung it on
the fridge. "We just need to buy a little time to get
everything squared away."

"Before he comes looking for me." She sighed. "He's not
stupid. He's going to see right through this. He's going to
find me, Lucien. And he's going to kill me." She gulped
down some air and stopped packing. Her hands shook. "I
can't do this. I can't."

Maybe this was a terrible idea, but staying with him
wasn't a good idea either. I searched the kitchen drawers
for a paper bag and folded over the sides. "Breathe into
this. You don't want to pass out. Just slow breaths in and
out." I had never seen anyone hyperventilate before, but I
had seen the bag trick on TV shows. Hopefully, that wasn't
creative licensing.

I rubbed her back softly, aware of the way she stiffened
at the physical contact. I was out of my depth. Pulling out
my phone, I dialed one of the area women's shelters and
stepped into the other room. Since I was no expert, I would
defer to someone who knew what to do.

"Who are you calling?" Jade asked, when she finally
calmed down enough to speak.

"The domestic abuse hotline."

Her already pale skin went stark white. "I can't go to one
of those places. I told you Scott's a cop. That's the first
place he'll look. He'll find me there. You can't take me to
one of those places. I won't go."

I put the phone down and held up my palms. "I know. I
just wanted to make sure we didn't forget to take
something you might need later. You need financial
documents, your bank account information, your credit
history, social security card, insurance cards, IDs." I
studied her. "Did he take any of those things away from
you?" According to the woman on the phone, the abuser
often turned his victim into a captive.

"No."

"All right. That's good. That'll make this easier." Though
Scott didn't have to resort to those measures since he had a
lot more resources at his disposal. He could probably trace

her cell phone or have someone pull up the GPS anti-theft tracking info on her vehicle. "As soon as we leave here, I'll get you a new cell phone. And I'll rent you a car at the airport."

"Where am I going to stay? What about work? I can't just skip town."

"Call in and tell them you have a family emergency. If they need documentation or proof, I'll get it for you."

"How?"

"Don't worry about that." I offered a reassuring smile. She finished packing her clothes and toiletries and whatever sentimental heirlooms she had. "How much of this furniture is yours?"

"Just the futon and that bookcase."

"What about the appliances or TV?"

She pointed to a small set on the kitchen counter. "That's mine."

"I'll buy you a new one once you get settled. What about the computer?"

"My laptop died three months ago. Scott's been letting me use his."

"Did you do any research on his computer that might be damning or lead him to believe the note is a lie?"

She shook her head.

"Where does your family live?"

"My dad's in Maryland. My mom's in Colorado."

"Does Scott know that?"

"I think so."

"Okay." I turned on the computer, searching for flight information. Then I looked up information on ischemic strokes and left the window minimized. With any luck, Scott would believe the lie. Since Jade had family in Maryland, I didn't want to risk leading Scott to them, so I checked flights to Portland, Maine. It might be enough to confuse him or at least delay him since they were both M states. "So this is everything?" I stared at the half a dozen duffel bags and two boxes.

"When I moved here, I only took what fit inside my car. My campus apartment came pre-furnished, and when I graduated, I moved in with Scott." The look in her eye told me she regretted that decision. She probably regretted ever coming to the city.

"Does he have access to your bank account?"

She shook her head. "No. We've always had separate accounts. He bought whatever we needed."

"Did you chip in on the rent?"

"He knew I didn't make enough for that. He said he wanted to take care of me." She snorted, her face dropping, and she glared at the recliner. "Asshole."

I checked the time. According to Jade, Scott wouldn't be home for hours, but I wanted to get Jade as far away from here as quickly as possible. "I'll load the car. Stay here until I'm done." For all I knew, Scott might have neighbors keeping watch. I didn't spot any surveillance cameras or security systems inside the apartment, but I couldn't be too careful.

Three trips later, I poked my head into the apartment. "Are you ready?"

She nodded, locking the door behind her and following me to the car. Once we were on the road, she let out the breath she'd been holding since we stepped foot inside the apartment. "What comes next?"

That's what I'd been asking myself this entire time. "First, we pick up your car and go to the airport. You're going to buy a plane ticket to Aunt Bonnie's." I saw the panic on her face. Flights were expensive, and she didn't have money to waste, especially to travel to see a fictitious aunt. "I'll reimburse you, just put it on your credit card in case Scott runs your financials. Once you get your plane ticket, I'll rent a car for you in my name. While I'm doing that, use the ATM to withdraw whatever cash you have remaining in your account. You won't be able to use your credit or debit cards after that."

I kept some emergency cash in a safe at the office. It would be enough to get her started. I pointed to the cell phone she held tightly in her hand. "Don't forget to call work."

"Right." Dazed, she lifted the phone and repeated the lie to her boss since that would be the first place Scott would go to verify her story. Overwhelmed, she hung up.

"Shouldn't I feel relieved?"

"You will once you realize you're free. This is the hard part. It should get easier after this. Right now, we just have to make sure you're safe and he can't find you."

FOUR

After leaving the airport, I brought Jade back to the office, handed her two hundred dollars in cash, and made some calls. She needed a safe place to stay, a place where Scott and the rest of his cop buddies wouldn't think to look for her. One day, Cross Security and Investigations would be equipped to deal with these types of situations, but my company wasn't there yet. Maybe I should have passed her off to someone more experienced, but I thought I could handle it. Now, I wasn't so sure.

Jade fidgeted. "Y'know, I spoke to a few other private eyes in the past. I didn't know where to go and thought, y'know, they could help. But they always passed me off to battered women's shelters or simply refused to take my case after they found out Scott was a police sergeant. Why aren't you doing the same thing?"

"I'm not that smart." I hung up the phone, relieved to have found shelter for Jade on such short notice. "Come on."

I stared through the windshield at the apartment building. Having a few friends in real estate made securing a place easier. Unfortunately, it didn't offer much in terms of security. The front door automatically locked, and visitors had to be buzzed in. But that was the extent of it. If Scott located her, he'd flash his badge and get inside the building. No one would stop him.

I unlocked the door and handed Jade the extra set of keys. "Here we are."

She stepped inside, looking around the empty apartment. "I don't know."

"It's fine. Let me get the rest of your things. Stay here. And stay out of sight."

On my way outside, I checked my messages. My assistant performed a background check on Jade to make sure she was who she claimed. Although I believed her story, I wasn't naïve enough to think I couldn't be conned by a damsel in distress. Wasn't that the plot of more than half the noir films I'd seen? Plus, certain people wanted me to fail. They wanted my latest endeavor to crash and burn, and this could be a creative way of making it happen. Or I was just paranoid.

Reassured Jade was as she appeared, I grabbed the rest of her belongings and locked the car. I rented the apartment under one of my LLCs to make it harder to trace. The rental car was under my name, so even if Scott came looking for her, he wouldn't find her. And I doubted he'd think to come after me. According to Jade, she saw an ad I had taken out on the back cover of a business magazine while at work and decided to stop by. No connection existed between the two of us, so Scott would never be the wiser.

"A medic needs to look at you." I put her boxes near the door. "We need documented proof of the abuse."

"No," she bit her lip and looked away, "I don't want that."

"We need it," I insisted. "It's bad enough there isn't a paper trail to establish repeat behavior, but one assault is more than enough."

"Yeah, but Scott knows people. He's friends with a lot of other first responders, paramedics, EMTs, even some of the people who work in the emergency room. He'll deny it, and they'll believe him."

"No, they won't." But I didn't know if that was true. "I

know some people who've used concierge medicine in the past. Let me see if I can get a name. I doubt any of those doctors rub elbows with law enforcement or first responders."

"How do you know so many people? Who are you? A long lost heir to the Rockefeller fortune?"

"I wish, but I'm just your average Joe."

"Somehow, I doubt that." Even though Jade had warmed to me, she kept her distance and wouldn't look me in the eye. She took her things and piled them in the corner, positioning herself near them like a dog guarding a bone. And I realized those material possessions were all she had left in the world.

After making some calls, several to my assistant, I put down the phone. "Furniture will be here tomorrow. Justin's bringing an air mattress and some freshly washed linens and towels for tonight. Grocery delivery is on the way. I just ordered basic staples. I didn't know if you were vegan."

"I'm not."

"Okay." I opened a cabinet, finding it empty. "I also ordered a set of stainless steel cookware, serving for four, dish soap, sponges, and things like that. Y'know, the basics. Tomorrow, you can make a list of whatever else you need, and I'll have someone deliver it. You have the car for emergencies, but I'd prefer if you stay here, at least for now."

She nodded, toying with the zipper on one of the duffel bags. "How long am I supposed to stay out of sight?"

I didn't have an answer. "I contacted a law firm, Reeves and Almeada. Have you heard of them?"

She shook her head.

"They take a lot of criminal cases. They know the ins and outs of the law. Mr. Almeada will meet with us tomorrow to go over your case."

"My case?"

"Yes. Scott needs to know you mean business and that he can't just push you around. Mr. Almeada will go over the steps you should take. Listen to him."

Jade sniffled. "I don't know. This is a mistake. I made a

mistake. I shouldn't be here." She looked at the cheap Timex on her wrist. "Maybe there's still time. I can go home. Put everything back where it was. He won't know."

"You can." Pushing her wasn't the answer. "But what happens if he comes home drunk or angry? What happens if you say something that sets him off? What is he going to do next time?" I studied her, the way she cowered and trembled. I'd seen people act like that before. It signaled the body was going into fight or flight. "It's up to you, Jade. It's your life. Your decision. Lots of abused individuals never leave their abusers. I'm not telling you you should." Though my actions spoke much louder than my words. "It's your call. You know how dangerous Scott is. You have to do what's best for you."

She looked up at me. "He will kill me one of these days. But being here gives him an excuse to do it sooner rather than later."

"I won't let him hurt you. He won't find you. And by the time he knows what's going on, he won't be in a position to hurt anyone ever again."

"Do you promise?"

"Yes."

She thought long and hard about everything. And then she cried.

FIVE

I slammed my palm against the steering wheel and blew into my closed fist, hoping to calm down. Right now, I felt like I might explode. I wanted to march into the police station and show Scott Renwin exactly what it felt like to be powerless and scared, but I wasn't crazy.

Instead, I waited in my car, staring at the clunky pickup. Obviously, Scott felt like a little man. That's why he needed to drive a big, powerful vehicle and why he thought it was a good idea to beat up on the weak. It might have also been what originally attracted him to join the police force – he craved power and authority. He didn't want to feel small or helpless, but by the time I was through with him, that's all he'd be.

At shift change, several officers, no longer in uniform, exited from the rear door. I spotted Scott; his face indelibly etched in my brain. He slapped one of his pals on the back, hollered something about meeting at KC's, and climbed into his truck. Revving the engine, he peeled out of the parking lot.

"You smug asshole." Checking the screen mounted to my dash, I watched the steady red blip move down the orange line. After his buddies drove off, I followed the tracker to the bar.

When I arrived at KC's, that eyesore of a truck caught my attention. I only recognized one other car from the police parking lot. Regardless, it was a cop bar, so starting a fight with a cop in front of a few dozen of his brothers-in-blue would result in unnecessary bloodshed. As in, my blood would be unnecessarily shed. Though the prospect might make Jade's claims more believable, it would tip our hand. And I didn't want to do that.

I stepped inside, squinting in the dim light. The bulk of the illumination came from the neon signs hanging behind the bar. I kept my eyes on the bartender, a grizzled, retired police lieutenant named Jim Harrelson. Scott leaned against one of the high-tops, sipping his beer. The foam left a white mustache on his upper lip.

"Hey, kid, what'll it be?" Jim asked.

I cleared my throat, my left eyebrow twitching. It had been a while since I stepped foot inside this place, but Jim didn't miss a trick. He remembered me.

"Gin."

Jim put down a glass, poured my preferred brand, and slid it toward me. "You lookin' for your pops?"

"Is he here?"

"Nope, hasn't been for a while."

I slid onto the stool, keeping an eye on Scott by using the reflection provided by the mirrored back wall. "He thinks he's too good for a place like this."

Jim shrugged. "I don't have a beef with your pops."

"That makes one of us."

The bartender didn't say anything. He wiped off the counter and moved to the other end to talk to some regulars. I hated this place. It made me twitchy and uncomfortable. And bad things happened whenever I got too twitchy. That was partially the reason I wasn't managing seven-figure accounts or trading on the floor anymore.

A glass broke, and I blinked, unsure if it just happened or if I was remembering the sound of sending my boss's desk chair careening through the window. I turned on my stool, finding a waitress kneeling down to pick up the shards. My gaze traveled up to Scott, who scowled while staring down at her. His fists involuntarily clenched.

Jim grabbed a broom and dustpan and stepped out from behind the bar to help her clean it up. From here, I couldn't make out their words, but the waitress hurried around the bar, filled a glass, and brought it back to Scott. He took it, nodded at the waitress, and turned back to the dartboard. Due to the angle, I didn't see exactly what happened, but from the annoyed look on the waitress's face, I suspected Scott had done something to cause her to drop the glass.

Scott's buddy laughed, slinging his arm around Scott's shoulder and clearly joking about something. Eventually, the pinched look disappeared from the bastard's face. He chugged down the rest of the beer, signaled to Jim, who was now back behind the bar, for another, and approached the dartboard.

For the next twenty minutes, I watched Scott and his friend take turns plucking the darts out of the board, throw them with terrible precision, and repeat the process until they ran out of beer. Scott looked at his watch, said his goodnights, and paid his tab. The asshole walked right past me, never noticing me, and clueless to the fact his entire world was about to turn upside down.

Once I was sure he was gone and wasn't coming back, I cornered the waitress when she took the trash out. "Hey, is everything okay?"

She narrowed her eyes, confused. "Sure." She glanced at the open side door, figuring if she screamed a dozen off-duty cops would rush to her rescue. Admittedly, she wasn't wrong, which meant I needed to make sure she didn't scream.

"I noticed the incident inside, but I didn't see what happened. Did Sergeant Renwin do something to you?"

Her gaze traveled up and down my body. I didn't have a badge or gun, like most of the guys inside. "Why do you ask?"

"Just curious."

She shook it off. "It's nothing new."

"What does that mean?"

"Hey, come on," she looked uncertainly back at the door, "it's nothing. Guys blow off steam. They think they're funny or cute. They want to show off to their friends. That's it."

"What did he do?" My voice sounded hard, like granite.

"He slapped my ass."

"Has he done it before?"

"Half the guys in there have done it before. It's nothing. But I wasn't expecting it. I got startled and dropped the beer. Enough said." Suddenly, something dawned on her. "Are you investigating Scott?" She scrutinized me more carefully, probably assuming I was with internal affairs. However, I doubted they dressed this nicely. They couldn't afford it on their salaries, unless they were on the take, which would defeat the entire purpose of IA.

"Perhaps. Can you think of any reason why someone should?"

"Nope." She slammed the lid on the dumpster. "Just be careful around here, Detective. No one likes a rat." She went back inside.

Realizing I made more of an impression than I intended, I got into my car and followed the red blip on my monitor back to Scott Renwin's apartment, wondering if she'd tell him about me the next time he stopped by for a drink. I parked halfway down the street, reached for my camera and the directional mic, and took a few snapshots while Scott threw a temper tantrum. I missed the initial explosion when he first arrived home and found Jade's note, but I knew there must have been one. He was a powder keg. It didn't take much to set him off. And I knew, after tonight, we were on a collision course. He just didn't know it yet.

SIX

I forwarded Jade's calls to my phone since her cell phone was in the airport parking lot. Since finding the note, Scott had called seven times. I listened to the messages again. Desperate, pleading, and angry. At first, he sounded concerned. He wanted to know where she went, when she'd be back, and what family member had fallen ill. He probably intended to drag her home, kicking and screaming. I didn't like it. I didn't like any of this.

According to the tracker I planted on Scott's rear bumper, he was at work now. But given the number of unreturned calls and texts, I didn't doubt he'd illegally use police resources to track her phone, her car, and her. I just hoped I covered all my bases.

"Mr. Cross?"

I looked up, tucking the phone back in my pocket. "Sorry."

The receptionist waved away my apology. "Please, if I had a dime for every time a client's been on the phone, I'd have millions." She jerked her head at her boss's office. "Mr. Almeada would like you to join them."

"Thanks." I stepped into the corner office, eyeing Jade who was curled up on one end of the couch. "How's it going in here?"

Mr. Almeada sighed. For an attorney, that was a bad sign. "It could be better, but I've seen worse. Ms. McNamara clearly has a case. The first thing we need to do is file a restraining order." Almeada's gaze flicked to Jade, who hugged her knees to her chest and stared at the floor. "Like I said, Scott Renwin won't be allowed within five hundred feet of you. That includes where you work, shop, eat, everything. If he violates the court order, he'll be held in criminal contempt and could be arrested. As I'm sure Mr. Cross has explained, the police department takes allegations of domestic abuse seriously. It's unlikely he'd risk opening himself up to an internal investigation by violating the terms of the court order."

"What if he doesn't care? What's to stop him from hurting me?" Jade asked.

"You'll have legal recourse," Almeada said, but that didn't satisfy her. I doubted that answer would satisfy anyone in her position.

"I will stop him." I glanced at Almeada, who was not pleased by my comment, but he'd already gone over the legal ramifications with her until he was blue in the face. A piece of paper wouldn't protect her from Scott's wrath. And she wanted assurances these measures would keep her safe. "I specialize in security. Someone will keep an eye out when you return to work. Scott won't get near you. I'll make sure of it."

"You don't need to worry about that yet," Almeada said. "You left safely. We'll get you set up with a post office box since addresses have to be on official court documents. Are you planning on staying here? Do you want to leave town? What do you want to do?"

Jade blinked. "I don't know."

"Okay. That's okay. You have time to think about it." I turned back to Almeada. "What happens to Scott?" Once approved, the restraining order would prohibit Scott from possessing a firearm, thus making it unlikely he'd be able to keep his job. The bastard fucked himself over when he decided it was okay to hit a woman. Unfortunately, that meant Jade's claims and case could cost Scott everything.

"I don't see why we would have any problems getting the restraining order, and I doubt we'll encounter any issues at the hearing. Of course, like I explained to Ms. McNamara, the restraining order won't go into effect until after the hearing. We could request a temporary order of protection until then. The department will probably start its own investigation into Jade's allegations once that's filed."

"Let's do that." I reached for my phone. "Send me a list of what we need to do in order to keep her hidden."

"No problem." Almeada made a note.

"What about pursuing criminal charges?" I asked.

Almeada looked at Jade. "Maybe you should talk to her about that."

I glared at the attorney. "I asked you a question. I'd like an answer."

Almeada snorted. He knew me well enough not to take offense. "The evidence is flimsy. No witnesses. No history of reported incidents. No hospital records or police reports to corroborate her claims. No neighbors calling to report anything suspicious. We have nothing except the doctor's report from last night and her word against his. He's a cop. Depending on what his record shows, the court is likely to find in his favor. The department might even find in his favor, so if he's willing to play by the rules, we might not need to take this further than a TRO. It'll depend on how vindictive Mr. Renwin chooses to be."

Jade shivered. "I don't know what he'll do."

"That's okay. Everything's going to be okay." Though I said the words, they sounded like hollow platitudes. "This can't be the first time he's done this. Others will come forward."

Almeada shrugged. "Digging into Renwin's background is in your wheelhouse. So I'll leave that up to you."

"I just want him to leave me alone. I don't want to push his buttons or piss him off. I want us to go our separate ways," Jade said. "I don't want to see him behind bars. I can't imagine that would be good for a police sergeant."

"It wouldn't, which is why he will think twice before hurting you again." I couldn't help thinking maybe she wasn't as over him as she claimed to be. Or she was a lot more forgiving than I was. My mind drifted to the waitress from last night. Renwin must have a history of violence and abuse. It was my job to dig it up.

"Until you learn more and we get the ball rolling on filing the court orders and getting a hearing on the books, the best thing I can tell you is to hurry up and wait," Almeada said. "You've taken the right first steps, Ms. McNamara." He glanced at me. "Mr. Cross might be new at this, but he knows his way around bypassing the system and dealing with criminal matters. I'd say you're in good hands."

Jade didn't appear to have heard a single word he said. She looked paler than usual. "I don't feel so well. Do you mind if I use your bathroom?"

Almeada pointed to a door visible through his glass office, and she ducked out, one hand clutching her stomach. "Nerves," Almeada surmised. "She's lucky. Based on her medical records and the report your doctor wrote, she hasn't suffered any permanent physical damage."

"She's not lucky. He's just careful." I stared out the door, fearing she might sneak out or bolt.

"Lucien," Almeada's tone caught my full attention, "let her do what she wants and what makes her comfortable. It's her life and her mistakes to make."

"She can't go back to him."

"I don't think she will. I've seen far too many cases like this. The ones who escape are determined. And she is. When you light a fire under her, you can see it. The determination. The grit. She'll get away, but she has to do it on her terms. Not yours."

"I wasn't..."

He clapped me on the shoulder. "Don't make your issues into her issues. She already has enough problems. Though, I am wondering why you decided to take this on. This isn't exactly your kind of case or client. You won't make a dime off this. If anything, you stand to lose quite a bit. Your company could crash and burn before it even gets off the ground. Are you prepared for that?"

"It's not always about the money. Don't you ever do

anything pro bono?"

"Yes, and those are always the ones that bite me in the ass."

SEVEN

"Now what?" Jade asked.

"Now we wait." I looked at the array of furniture that had been delivered while we were out and gave her Justin's number. "If you need anything else, text my assistant. He'll get back to you within the hour."

"Where are you going?"

I turned, unsure if she was afraid to stay by herself. "You're safe. You didn't have any problems last night after I left, did you?"

"It's not that." She took a seat at the kitchen table. "I just don't know what to do."

"I'm sure you'll figure something out, but please, don't leave the apartment until after the hearing."

"Yeah, okay."

I offered an encouraging smile. "Like I said, if you need something, Justin will bring it to you. You met him yesterday. He was the guy messing with the phones."

"Right."

"Okay. I'll be in touch if I have any questions."

"Can I call you?" she asked, a begging quality to her tone that pulled at something inside of me.

"Of course."

She smiled. "I'll see you later."

Confused by the exchange, I wrote it off as a hazard of working with non-corporate entities and returned to the car. This case was personal to Jade and to me too. Though I wasn't entirely sure why I found myself so invested. It didn't matter. What mattered was keeping Scott Renwin from hurting Jade or anyone else. And the first place to start was the precinct.

Before stepping foot inside, I checked the time. My mouth went dry, and my stomach muscles clenched. Sucking it up, I pulled on the door handle and entered the police station. A couple of people were speaking to an officer and a detective in the back corner. I ignored them and approached the desk.

The white-haired desk sergeant absently hummed as she pecked away at the keys. I cleared my throat, waiting for her to look up. "Just a sec," she said. The ancient printer on the counter behind her beeped and devoured the blank paper from the tray, spitting it back out a second later. She picked it up, stamped it, and stuck it in a folder before looking up.

"Are you ready yet? Or should I come back?"

A smile tugged at her lips. "Lucien, quit sassing your elders." She put her hands on the counter and stared at me. "Look at you in that fancy suit. Have you gotten taller?" She leaned over the counter to look at my shoes.

"What are you doing?"

"Just wondering if you're wearing lifts."

"Come on, Sara. Do you really think I need another inch or two?"

She quirked an eyebrow at me.

"The answer is no." I glared at her, even though I had nothing but affection for the woman.

She straightened. "You look good. I don't think I've seen you since your academy days. When was that? Three years ago?" She sobered. "Tough break, but it looks like it worked out for the best. The last I heard you were doing something with stocks." Her forehead crinkled. "At least you put those computer science and economics degrees to use."

"Unfortunately, I'm not doing that anymore either. I got blackballed after squealing on my boss for embezzling." Among other things.

"I'm surprised the SEC didn't offer you a job."

"Why would they? I have a record."

"I thought the assault was expunged."

"Still."

"Cut the crap. I don't want to hear any of this 'woe is me' bullshit. You wouldn't be dressed like that if life was crap. Did you come back just to rub it in our faces?"

"I wouldn't do that."

She snorted. "Who the hell are you kidding?"

I tilted my head to the side, considering her words. "Well, I wouldn't do that to you."

She stared at me for a moment before accepting it as true. I had plenty of reasons to despise the police department, but Sgt. Sara Rostokowski was a good and decent woman. I wouldn't take my bias out on her just because she wore a uniform.

She crooked her finger, like she wanted to tell me a secret. "You were always too good for the uniform, Lucien. Even if you made it through the academy, you wouldn't have stuck around long. The Feds would have swooped in and stolen you the first chance they got."

"Whatever."

She growled, deep in her throat. "Regardless, you're definitely too good to be rubbing elbows with snakes and weasels on Wall Street. Your father wants better for you. So what are you doing now? What brings you here today?"

I scoffed and stared at the recruitment poster on the wall. Lies. It was nothing more than propaganda and lies. The police department claimed to have standards, but they let assholes like Scott Renwin into their ranks. My blood pressure spiked, and I shoved my hands into my pockets before they turned into fists. "Security and investigations."

"Private?"

"Yes."

"Where are you working?"

"Cross Security and Investigations." The smugness crept

into my voice.

She whistled. "Bet your father loves that."

"He doesn't know." Shifty-eyed, I stepped closer to the desk and lowered my voice. "I could use your help. I need a favor."

She glanced around and leaned closer. "What do you need?"

"Sergeant Scott Renwin's records. Anything you can find. Civilian complaints, evaluations, a psych profile. I'll take whatever you have."

"You're investigating a cop? Are you insane? What do you think this guy did?"

I licked my lips. I didn't want to say. "Will you help me? No one can know about this."

"Damn right, no one can know about this. I don't need my ass in a sling." She made sure no one was within earshot. "But I'll see what I can do. Where can I send the records?" I picked up a pen and wrote down instructions on how to access my online dropbox. She tucked the note into her pocket and patted me on the shoulder. "Be careful, kid. I don't know what you've gotten yourself into, but it sounds like you're playing with fire. Your old man won't like it."

"I don't need his approval." I shook off the resentment. "Take care of yourself, Sara. This place does things to good people."

"Maybe that's why I'm sticking around." She grinned. "Someone has to keep these officers and detectives in line."

"Truer words."

I went back to the car and deflated in the seat. Aside from hacking into the police servers, I had done everything I could to get Renwin's service records. Sara would do her best. In the meantime, I'd find whatever dirt I could on Renwin.

EIGHT

Rubbing a hand down my face, I stared at the computer screen. It had taken quite a bit of work and more effort than necessary, but I found plenty on Scott Renwin. I knew where he was born, who his best friend was in kindergarten, his GPA in high school, how he paid someone to write his college essays for him, and how he scraped by until he was accepted into the police academy. None of that was useful.

I dug deeper until I compiled a list of women he dated over the years, from high school until now. None of them ever filed a report or took out a TRO or protection order against him. I sent the list to my assistant, hoping he might convince one of the women to give up some dirt I missed.

As far as I could tell, Jade was the first woman he lived with besides his mother. I spoke to Mrs. Renwin, but she only had the fondest things to say about her son. When I asked about her late husband, she said he was a good provider, which read to me like he'd used his wife and maybe Scott as punching bags, but I didn't have any proof. Though, it would explain the cycle of violence.

"Dammit." I picked up Scott's bank account information. He had enough to be comfortable without raising any eyebrows. His monthly expenses didn't fluctuate aside from the occasional unexpected purchase, like new tires for his truck. From what I could tell, he didn't do much except work, drink, and beat up Jade. Scott kept a low-profile, which would make things more difficult. Right now, it was her word against his, but I knew Scott had done this before. This couldn't be the first time. And if someone didn't put an end to his reign of terror, it wouldn't be the last.

Dialing Almeada, I put the phone on speaker and stared out my door into the reception area. My receptionist had been on the phone most of the day, scheduling interviews and appointments. Cross Security had been in the midst of hiring computer experts and a platoon of security specialists when Jade walked into my life. I needed to get at least eight security specialists who could work guard duty and two or three computer techs before signing contracts with my corporate clients on Monday. Now wasn't the time to take a domestic abuse case. I was already hemorrhaging money, and Jade McNamara wasn't even a paying client.

"What the fuck are you doing, Lucien?" I muttered.

"Shouldn't I ask you that?" Almeada said, having answered sometime during my internal monologue.

"Probably." I filled the attorney in on the progress I made. "What have you found on your end? Did you discover anything substantial to hold against Renwin?"

"Cross, you aren't listening. Ms. McNamara doesn't want to pursue criminal charges. She doesn't want to file any additional claims against her boyfriend. She just wants him to leave her alone. She only wants a restraining order and assurances he won't violate it. This might never go beyond a TRO. Frankly, that would probably be in everyone's best interest. It would allow Renwin the greatest chance of keeping his job, and Ms. McNamara can move on. As long as he has something to lose, he'll be less likely to violate the court order."

"But this is how we make sure he doesn't violate it," I said, exasperated.

"You're going to blackmail him into submission? That's your plan?"

I hadn't thought of it in those terms. "He needs to know if he touches her again, his life will blow up."

"That's a guarantee if he violates the court order," Almeada said patiently. "The mailbox is set up. I have the paperwork ready to go. I'll send it out in the morning."

"Okay."

Almeada didn't hang up. "Your okay doesn't sound very okay."

"I said okay." Annoyed, I disconnected.

According to the tracker, Renwin's truck was at the precinct. Since he had a steady schedule, I had time to do more digging. So I went back to KC's. The place was crowded with the men and women who'd come off second shift, but I found an empty seat in the corner.

Jim looked surprised to see me again. "We don't stock the best quality gin here."

"Tell me about it." I watched as he poured from a bottle.

"If you're planning on making this your usual haunt, you better let me know. I'll order something that won't burn the hair off your chest." He smirked. "Although, a pretty boy like you probably manscapes."

"I didn't know you knew words like manscape."

He shoved the glass toward me. "So is this gonna be a regular thing?"

"If it is, I'll switch to beer."

Jim rolled his eyes. "Let me guess. You want a fancy import."

"Is that the cop instinct I hear so much about?"

He glanced down the bar to make sure no one needed anything. "What are you doing here, Lucien? Melody said you were asking about Scott Renwin. She thinks you're heading an internal investigation."

"I never said I was a cop. That would be illegal."

"Like you give a shit about that." His sigh sounded like a growl. "What the hell are you doing?"

"It doesn't concern you."

"It's my bar. That makes it my concern." He pointed to a sign on the back wall. "And I can refuse service to anyone."

"I thought you were going to special order my preferred brand of gin. That doesn't sound like you're refusing service." I stared straight-faced at him. "Is this because I drink imported beer?" I didn't like asking for things, especially help. And I didn't know how to ask questions without tipping my hand. This was a bad idea.

"You cocky shit. Answer the damn question."

I bit back the smartass response dancing on my tongue. I didn't know where Jim Harrelson's loyalties lay. "The waitress looked scared. Scott slapped her ass. I didn't like it, so I asked her about it. That was it."

"He touched her?"

"According to her, a lot of the men have gotten out of hand a time or two. She doesn't appreciate it. Looks like you've created an unsafe work environment." I glanced at the other waitresses. "I'm guessing the others probably have similar stories."

"Yeah, but you asked specifically about Scott."

"He's the only one I saw."

Jim's eyes narrowed. "I'll keep an eye out and tell the staff to report inappropriate behavior immediately."

"They probably won't say anything. It could impact their tips."

But Jim was a dog with a bone. "How'd you know Scott's name?"

"Must have heard someone say it." I met him glare for glare. "Since you're so hung up on the jerk, I'm wondering why. Does the bastard typically give you problems?"

Jim reached beneath the bar. For a moment, I wondered if he planned to pull out a shotgun and tell me to leave. But that would have been melodramatic, especially since he was practically my uncle. He slapped a magazine down on the bar, the back cover facing up with my Cross Security ad staring at us. "Tell me what you've gotten yourself into, son."

"Nothing."

"Renwin drinks too much. I take his keys away at least twice a month. Most of the time, someone drives him home. One night, I found him passed out in the men's room. I called his girlfriend to come get him." Jim studied my expression, but I remained impassive. I spent most of my life making sure my face never gave anything away, unless I wanted it to. "I helped her drag him out to the car. It was dark. So I might have been mistaken."

"What did you see?"

He wiped the bar. "You need to be careful. You're not just fucking with a man's private life. He's a cop. Things like this could end his career."

"Whatever happens, he did it to himself. People like that shouldn't be able to carry guns or terrorize the innocent."

"I didn't say they should. All I said is you need to be careful. He won't like some private dick poking around in his business."

"I don't care. I need to find evidence."

"Scott's girl should be covered in it."

"Nothing's ever been documented. No police reports or 9-1-1 calls. Scott could say someone else did it." I looked at Jim in a new light. "Unless you happened to witness something."

"Like I said, it was dark."

"Bullshit." I drained the rest of the glass and flipped it over. It was time to leave. "If this goes to court, we could subpoena you."

Jim snorted. "I'm an unreliable witness."

"So you won't help?"

"I didn't say that. I'm just saying I know how these things work." Jim glanced around again, but no one was close to us. "You need to go to your pops. He'll take care of it."

"I'd rather be mauled by wild dogs."

NINE

For the next few days, I checked my dropbox to the point of obsession and toyed with the idea of phoning Sara. As a desk sergeant, she had access to a lot of information, and since she'd been with the department for more than twenty years, she could get me what I wanted. So why was my dropbox empty?

My phone chimed an alert, and I picked it up. Renwin's truck was on the move. Scott had finally gotten tired of leaving frantic and slightly threatening voicemails and text messages and decided to go to the airport. Frankly, I was surprised it had taken him this long. He had every reason to be concerned about Jade's well-being and that of her sick aunt, but after the initial messages he left, the situation devolved.

The last thirty texts alternated between begging Jade to come back and threatening her with what he'd do if she didn't listen. That wasn't what a supportive partner should do, which told me one thing. He knew she left him. And he knew why. By now, he must have received notice of the impending court hearing and realized he was running out of time. If Jade didn't withdraw the claim, things would progress. And Scott's life would end up under the microscope.

I grabbed my jacket and glanced down at my private investigator's license that I'd received this afternoon. It had taken some cajoling to get the process expedited, but I was now licensed by the state. But on the off chance Scott confronted me, I didn't want him to know that. So I left the wallet-sized card on my desk, asked the receptionist to redirect my calls to my cell, and told my assistant to conduct the rest of the interviews this afternoon. Then I slid behind the wheel and followed Scott to the airport.

When I arrived, his giant truck was double-parked behind Jade's car. I slowed to the posted speed limit, flipped on my lights, and circled around until I found a space that allowed me to glimpse the level below. I cut the engine and reached for the camera beside me.

Scott waited as a few more cars entered in search of long-term parking. When the coast was clear, he removed the coat hanger from inside his jacket and popped the lock. Obviously, he didn't have a set of keys to Jade's car.

He slid into the front seat and found her cell phone in the cupholder. She told me that's where she normally kept it when driving, and he might think she forgot it. I watched him through the viewfinder as he attempted to turn on the dead phone, getting the dying battery signal before the device automatically powered off. After that, he searched the rest of her car, popped the trunk, and checked everywhere. I couldn't hear him from this distance, but I could read lips. He cursed and swore.

He slammed the trunk lid, rubbing a hand over his mouth. He went back into the car, pocketed her cell phone, and tapped anxiously on the dashboard. He knew she was gone. He also knew she'd be back. By now, he'd received notice of her intentions. If Jade pressed the issue for a permanent restraining order and the judge ruled in her favor, Scott would be prohibited from possessing a firearm. He'd lose his job. He'd lose everything. And that's why he so desperately wanted to stop her. He didn't realize his actions only made things worse.

With her cell phone in his pocket, he checked the car one last time before circling around the garage until he found a space. I remained inside my car, the camera hidden out of sight, while he stormed past. He hung his badge around his neck, and I waited until he entered the elevator before I got out of my car and took the stairs down, following him into the airport.

While I browsed the newsstand, I kept an eye on him while he spoke to a ticket agent. He flashed his credentials. Eventually, airport security and TSA agents stepped in to assist. Law enforcement lived by a code, so after hearing Scott's sob story, they believed he was genuinely concerned about his girlfriend and shared her flight information and failure to board with him. Now he knew she hadn't left the city. And from the look on his face, the shit was about to hit the fan.

He held it together, thanked them for their kindness, and left the airport. I bought a messenger bag, paid with the cash in my pocket, and checked the blip on my phone. Scott hadn't left yet. Donning my sunglasses, I took off my jacket, put it in the bag, and slipped it across my chest before exiting.

The bastard stood just outside the sliding doors. He paced back and forth, squeezing Jade's phone in his hand. He didn't know what to do. I kept my head down and waited at the crosswalk. Once it was clear, I crossed to the parking garage.

Half a dozen people waited for the elevator, and I stood near them, shifting from foot to foot. When the doors opened, we squeezed inside. Right before the doors closed, a hand pushed against them. The doors automatically slid apart, and Scott entered. He sidestepped around the luggage, pressing in beside me.

He gave me an odd look, but I left my sunglasses on, giving him a slight head nod. "It's good to be home, huh?" I mumbled.

Scott didn't answer, losing interest in me as he waited for the doors to open. Once they did, he stepped out, along with two other people. I remained inside, watching him trudge toward his truck as the doors closed. They opened again a moment later, and I stepped out and circled around to my car. By the time I got inside, Scott had pulled away.

I called Almeada. "He knows she's in the city."

"He received notice this morning."

"That explains it." I stared at Jade's car. "I'm on my way to the apartment to tell her what's going on. She needs to be prepared."

"Do you think Sgt. Renwin will be smart about this?"

Nothing about Scott's behavior led me to believe he ever made a smart decision, but he didn't have a record. No one ever filed any complaints against him, and as far as I knew, all of his ex-girlfriends were alive and breathing. Hopefully, he'd do the right thing and let Jade go without putting up too much of a fight. But something told me he wouldn't. "This will royally fuck him over. He wants to stop this before it buries him. That's why he's desperate to get to her. We have to keep her safe. We have to keep him away from her."

"Do you think he wants to negotiate?" Almeada asked. "If he agrees to her terms behind closed doors, we can enter into an agreement that won't cost him his job."

"It's too late for that." I remembered the fear in Jade's eyes when she talked about him. "He's going to violate the terms the moment we turn our backs. I know it. Jade knows it. That's why she's so afraid."

"If you're right, this is gonna get messy."

"It already is." I hung up and headed to Jade's.

TEN

I stayed at Jade's that night, though she didn't know it. Telling her Scott had gone to the airport and knew she hadn't left the city left her visibly shaken. I downplayed the situation, repeating the things Mr. Almeada had said. But Jade truly believed Scott would kill her. And with the resources of the police department at his disposal, she couldn't just disappear. He'd find her and drag her back, or he'd bury her. That's why she had to take official action.

A permanent restraining order would cost him his job. But her request for a TRO would put him on law enforcement's radar. Should anything happen to her, he'd be their prime suspect. And he spent enough years on the force to know it. That might just be her saving grace. It's what we were counting on, but Scott was unpredictable.

Drunk or angry, he'd lash out. I saw the unstable moodiness in the concealed rage Scott attempted to hide at the airport and the way he acted toward Melody, the waitress. Sure, Scott knew how to put on a good front, and most people didn't look too hard. But I wasn't most people. Call it a talent or super power, but I saw people for who they were. And given how volatile Scott's mood swings were, it could go either way.

Unfortunately, Scott left Jade with no other choice. At

least none that I could see. Even Mr. Almeada agreed. So here I was, camped out in my car with a gun on the seat beside me. If someone told me a year ago this is what I'd be doing on a Thursday night, I'd say he was crazy. Now, it didn't seem so crazy.

Justin sent me the list of applicants, and I scrolled through their names and qualifications. I needed to hire trained security personnel ASAP. Former military, former law enforcement, former SpecOps, each individual was qualified, but I was concerned with why they no longer collected government paychecks. I didn't need to hire anyone unbalanced, but gaining access to psychological evaluations could be difficult. Fortunately, I didn't mind breaking a few rules.

Years spent studying computer science afforded me connections to some of the least known and best hackers around. Though I knew creatively coloring outside the lines shouldn't be something I did on a regular basis, this was an emergency. Jade needed a competent and loyal team to guard her until the dust settled, and I needed to have a few teams waiting in the wings for my corporate clients.

Hiring ten tacticians would serve my immediate purposes. I selected the top candidates from the applicant pool and did most of my own research. After weeding out a few questionable characters, I sent the remaining names to a friend, along with the promise of payment in untraceable bitcoin. I'd have answers by the morning, so I sent a message to my assistant to draft the employment contracts and to have someone from Reeves and Almeada make sure they were airtight. By tomorrow afternoon, Cross Security would finally get off the ground.

Finished with that, I reread the tech applications. Personally, I didn't have any qualms with hiring a computer nerd with a non-violent record, but it could open my company up to liability issues. I didn't need the extra headache. Plus, the best computer whizzes never got caught. And I only wanted to hire the best. However, the best were bright enough to create their own billion-dollar internet startups and didn't need me. And the ones who lacked ambition already had jobs in Silicon Valley. Maybe I would have to go with second best.

Since I didn't have to make a decision right away, I made a note to ask Almeada about ways to indemnify myself from fallout should I hire former hackers to work internet security. When I finished making up for spending the afternoon out of the office, I leaned back in my seat and stared at the apartment building. Most of the lights were off, but I could see one light on in Jade's apartment. Did she fear the dark?

I thought about calling and asking if she was okay, but she already had enough men stalking her. So I listened to the radio for a while and stared at the red blip on my phone. Scott's truck was parked at his place. He didn't go to KC's. That surprised me. I thought he'd want a drink after the day he had, but maybe he was throwing a few back at home.

I got out of my car and stretched my legs, stopping by a twenty-four hour convenience store to grab coffee and a snack. On my way back to the car, my phone chimed. Surprised by the notification, I tripped on the sidewalk, spilling the coffee on my shirt. "Shit."

Wiping my phone on my pants, I entered my passcode and logged into my dropbox. A dozen PDF files filled my screen. Thank you, Sara.

I locked my doors, glanced around, and opened Sgt. Scott Renwin's performance evaluation. Scott was a mediocre cop. He did his job. No more. No less. He squeaked by on most things, but Scott's biggest problems, as noted in his evaluation, were his attitude and the number of complaints against him.

Opening the next file, I read the civilian complaints lodged against him. Excessive force. Belligerent. Disrespectful. Those three phrases repeated themselves over and over. My fingers cramped, and I made the conscious effort to relax my grip on the phone, not realizing how infuriated I had become. The police department knew Scott was an unstable powder keg, but they didn't do anything about it. But I would.

After sending copies to Almeada, I called Sara Rostokowski. Since she just uploaded the PDFs an hour ago, she should be awake. Plus, it was almost dawn, or it would be in a couple of hours. Maybe she was an early riser. Or she picked up a late shift. It didn't matter. I needed to talk to someone.

"I didn't think you'd be up," she said.

"Is that why you waited so long to send the files?"

"No," she sounded remorseful, "it took longer than I thought to access them. They were spread out."

"Yeah." I noticed the dates. This had been going on for three years, roughly around the same time Jade said Scott first hit her. "Did you find anything from before?"

"No."

"So he just woke up one day and turned into an asshole?"

"It looks that way."

"How come no one in the department's done anything about it?"

"I don't know. The incidents were evaluated. Scott was reprimanded on a few. On the others, the findings were inconclusive. If I had to guess, he probably doesn't have enough strikes against him."

I rubbed my eyes. "That's bullshit."

"He never hurt anyone, not to the level the department or city would face penalties, so the brass recommended some anger management and refused to bump up his pay until his performance evaluations improved. That's about it. You know, civilians file false claims all the time."

"These aren't false."

"Maybe not, but that's why we have union reps. Someone has to protect us from the vindictive assholes."

"In this case, your union is protecting a vindictive asshole. Is IA looking into it?"

"They are now," Sara said, and I knew she was the cause.

"Thanks. They'll be getting a lot more information soon."

ELEVEN

"Hey, boss," Justin said when I walked into the office a little after six a.m. "What happened to you?"

I looked down, remembering the spilled coffee from hours ago. "Remind me to keep a change of clothes at the office."

"I'll pick up your dry cleaning in an hour, unless you want to go home and shower. Maybe get some sleep too."

"That can wait." The background checks came back on my potential hires, and I wanted to get the paperwork done. "Here's the list of security personnel I want on the payroll. Let's get the offer letters and contracts drafted and schedule meetings, the sooner the better." I checked the calendar. I had four meetings scheduled with prospective corporate clients on Monday. Two in the morning, a lunch meeting, and one in the afternoon. Jade's court appearance was Monday, but Almeada would handle that. "Bring me Amir Karam's application."

"But he's a tech expert."

"I know that." I stared at Justin, wondering why he suddenly thought he should question me.

"Yes, sir."

As I perused Mr. Karam's qualifications, I left a

voicemail for Almeada. This was the fourth one I left in the last six hours, but I had questions and since I shelled out the attorney's exorbitant retainer fee every month, he would get over it. Last night, I decided I could wait to hire IT experts since I could do most of the work myself or source it out without anyone being the wiser, but in the light of day, with corporate clients on the horizon and being stretched too thin, it couldn't wait.

Unlike the other applicants, Amir didn't just have a computer background. He also had a science background with an emphasis in forensics. The former NSA analyst turned college professor just finished a stint teaching evidence collection and analysis at the FBI academy in Quantico. He'd be perfect, but when I initially tried to woo him, he wasn't impressed by Cross Security. He wanted fancy lab equipment and top of the line technology, not an espresso maker hidden away in what was once a closet turned break room. But maybe I could persuade him to change his mind.

At seven, when my receptionist arrived at work, she silently made me a cappuccino, placed it beside me, and went back to her desk. I blinked a few times, rereading the proposal I drafted. It wasn't much since the only numbers I had to play with were projections based on guesswork. I had no idea how many clients I'd sign or how much work they'd pass my way. When I embarked on this endeavor, eighteen of my former clients expressed an interest in working with Cross Security. But until they signed the paperwork, those were nothing more than hollow promises. Still, it was something to go on.

I hit print and handed the paper copy to my receptionist. "Read over this and tell me what you think. Mark any suggestions or changes on here, and I'll look them over."

She nodded, just as the phone rang. "Cross Security and Investigations. How may I help you?"

I went back to my desk, my eyelids pulsing to the beat of my heart. Almeada hadn't called back yet, but he rarely showed up to work before nine. A few minutes later, the door opened, and one of the men I hoped to hire stepped inside. Spit-shined and sharp, he gave his name to the receptionist. Before he even sat down, I stepped into the doorway, doing my best to appear in charge, despite my coffee-stained shirt, unshaved face, and tired eyes.

"Thanks for coming in so quickly. Please." I gestured into my office and the man followed me inside. Since he showed up before my attorney had time to review the contracts, I considered stalling, but I already appeared unprepared. Waiting would only make it worse. "I'm pleased to extend an offer to you." I handed him the paperwork, relieved when Justin appeared in my doorway with some clean clothes. "I'll give you a few minutes to look over the terms."

Getting up, I took my dry cleaning into the tiny bathroom and changed. After changing and combing my hair, I went back into my office and signed the first member of my security team. Just nine more to go.

Almeada phoned around 9:30 to say the contracts were solid, which was a relief since I had already signed two new employees while I waited for him to get out of bed and get to work. My assistant made miracles happen. Admittedly, it didn't hurt that these former military types routinely woke at five a.m. for the hell of it. As soon as my prospective new hires received Justin's call, they headed to my office. Why didn't everyone behave this way? *Patience, Lucien.*

Aside from the contracts being solid, Almeada also said he needed more time to review Scott Renwin's files, but he wanted to subpoena Renwin's records to keep things official and aboveboard, particularly now that he knew doing so would be worthwhile.

"Great," I said.

"Have you spoken to any of the people who filed complaints against Sgt. Renwin?"

"Not yet." It was on my list of things to do, somewhere between getting a team ready for on-the-job training and catching some zzz's.

"All right. When you do, let me know. Proceedings like this don't require witnesses, but I like to be prepared."

"That's why I like you."

"That's why? I thought it was because I saved your ass from serving hard time."

"You aren't my only phone-a-friend. But that didn't hurt either."

"Cross," Almeada said, "do you have any idea what triggered Renwin's change in behavior?"

"Not yet." Though, it was another thing on my to-do list. "I'll ask Jade if she remembers what happened around the time he changed. Most times, a break like that would be caused by a traumatic event, maybe a death." Scott's unresolved issues with dear old dad could have manifested in the son turning into his father. But I didn't want to speculate, nor did I care. What turned Scott into a monster wasn't my fault or my job to figure out or fix. My only concern was keeping him away from Jade. The police department would have to figure out a way to keep him away from the general public. That was beyond the scope of my capabilities.

Hanging up, I opened my office door and invited the next future Cross Security employee inside. He had just signed on the dotted line when my receptionist came to the door. She knew not to disturb me unless it was urgent.

"What is it?" I asked her.

"Ms. McNamara's on the phone. She said the cops are outside her door."

TWELVE

I raced to Jade's, leaving Justin in charge of the contract negotiations. He knew how far I was willing to go to sign these men and women, but it made me itchy not handling it myself. It was my name on the line. This was Cross Security and Investigations. And I was Lucien fucking Cross. But none of that mattered right now.

Driving past the apartment building, I noted the two patrol cars parked near the front door. No lights. No sirens. I wrote down the cruiser numbers, found the closest space a block away, and jogged back to Jade's building. Entering the code, I stepped inside.

It took time for my eyes to adjust to the dim hallway, and I nearly tripped on the stairs. I didn't have a plan. I couldn't even remember if I grabbed my wallet on the way out. My carry permit and P.I. license were inside. I'd need them if things went south.

I burst onto Jade's floor. The stairwell door banged against the wall, and a uniformed officer turned to look in my direction. His hand rested on his holster, but his posture didn't appear threatening. He offered a tight smile and nodded.

I returned the gesture and went past him down the hall to Jade's apartment, noticing his partner speaking to a man inside the apartment. Without knocking, I slipped my copy of the key into the lock and turned the knob.

"Hey, it's Lucien," I called, pulling the door closed behind me and relocking the door. "Jade? Hello?"

Her things remained in the corner of the room, but I didn't see her. Reaching into my pocket, I pulled out my phone and dialed her new number. I waited, listening. A moment later, the annoying high-pitched melody played.

"Jade?" I tried again. "Are you in here? It's only me. I didn't mean to barge in." I glanced out the window in case she decided to take her chances on the ledge. Where could she be? I cleared my throat. "Jade?" The car keys remained on the kitchen counter.

Knocking on the bedroom door, I waited a second before twisting the knob. It was locked, which could only be done from the inside. She had to be here. I knocked louder. Still nothing.

A sick thought twisted my stomach in knots. What if he found her? What if he locked the two of them in her bedroom? Maybe the cops in the hallway were his lookouts.

"Jade?" I said more frantically, though my volume remained low. I didn't want anyone outside the apartment to hear what was going on. It's why I didn't knock on the door before letting myself in.

I turned around and mule-kicked the door. The cheap lock gave way under the force, and I pulled my gun and stepped into the bedroom.

She didn't scream. Why didn't she scream? I swept the room. No one was here, but I heard a whimper coming from the bathroom.

Oh god. For a moment, I thought I might have a heart attack. Sweat coated my skin, dripping into my eyes. I wiped it away with the back of my hand. Another strangled whine came from inside, making me forget everything. The sound grabbed me, and I shouldered my way through the locked bathroom door, gun aimed.

Her teal eyes went wide. Tears dripped down her face, and she pressed both her hands even harder against her lips, muffling the surprised scream. I looked around, barely able to breathe. She eased one of her hands off her mouth, fighting not to sob.

"Whoa, hey," I said, seeing the gun in my hands and realizing it shouldn't be there. Tucking it into my holster, I held up my palms, which shook. "I'm sorry. I didn't mean to point the gun at you. I won't hurt you. You know that. I didn't mean to startle you. My receptionist gave me your message, and when I tried calling back, you didn't answer. I didn't know what happened. I thought..."

She trembled, biting her fist to muffle her shrieks and sobs. I looked around the bathroom. I didn't know what happened or why she locked herself inside. At the moment, nothing made sense. Dropping to my knees beside the tub, I rested my elbow on the ledge and took a few deep breaths.

By the time Jade calmed down, my heart rate had dropped to something that probably wouldn't even register on a monitor. People always accused me of being heartless. Maybe this was why.

She sniffled and wiped her eyes, still shaky. "What are they doing here?"

"Who?"

"The police." She swallowed, wincing. Her throat sore from the sobs and screams. "They knocked on my door and asked if I'd seen a man. They wanted to know if I was alone. They wanted to come inside."

"Did you recognize them? Are they Scott's friends?"

"I don't know. I was so scared." She placed her hand on the tub ledge, and I inched mine forward until it brushed against hers. She stretched her fingers out and took my hand. "I told them I didn't know anything and had something on the stove, so they couldn't come in. After that," the tears silently fell, "I just hid in the tub like I always do when Scott's on a tear. He's like a tornado."

"So you take cover in the tub?" I teased. "Makes sense."

She laughed, probably from nerves. "It's stupid. But I figured they'd tell him I was here. I thought by hiding in the bathtub he wouldn't be able to find me."

"I'm sorry." I stood, reaching down to help her out of the tub, though my own legs wobbled. "I didn't mean to scare you. You didn't answer the phone. And I didn't want to attract unnecessary attention by knocking on your door. Why didn't you answer when I called your name?"

"I didn't hear you, just the bedroom door slamming. Another thing Scott does frequently." She scowled, stepping out of the tub. The soles of her sneakers squeaked as she slipped on the tile. Automatically, I enveloped her in my arms to stop her from falling, and she tensed. "I'm sorry. I'm so clumsy."

"Don't apologize. Never apologize."

She pushed against my chest. "In that case, let go." She didn't like to be touched.

I slowly released her, making sure her footing was stable. "Most accidents happen in the bathroom. Let's get out of here so I can figure out what's going on without having to worry about one of us falling and breaking our neck."

We went back into the living room, and I peered through the peephole. The police officers had moved on to another apartment. They were canvassing the building. I just didn't know why. It made me uneasy.

"Stay here. I'll be right back."

She swallowed, aghast at the prospect, but managed to say, "Okay."

I buttoned my jacket and opened the door. "Excuse me," I said to the officer who acknowledged me earlier. "Do you mind if I ask what's going on? My roommate said you dropped by to ask her about a man."

The officer nodded and flashed a photo in my direction. "An hour ago, this man broke into the ATM down the street. Eyewitnesses say they thought they saw him enter one of these apartment buildings. Have you seen him?"

I looked at the photograph, a blown-up image from the ATM's surveillance camera. "No, sir. I was at work."

"Yeah, I figured as much. With the buzzer on the door, I bet he entered the other apartment building, but we have to be thorough. In case you see him, please call 9-1-1 and let them know."

"Absolutely."

THIRTEEN

"Did you give them your name?" I asked.

"No, of course not."

"Good." I tapped my phone against the table. "And you didn't recognize either of them?"

Jade shook her head.

"Okay, let me make a few calls and see if dispatch received reports and sent the two patrol units to check it out."

"How are you going to do that?" Jade asked.

I smirked. "Magic."

Sara Rostokowski wasn't my only friend in the department. I had several, even a few in dispatch. After verifying the details, I hung up and peered out the window. An evidence collection van parked down the street, and another two blue and whites arrived to rope off the area surrounding the ATM. The call appeared legit.

"Lucien, I'm sorry I bothered you."

Confused, I turned to look at her. "You have no reason to apologize." Returning to the front door, I peered out the peephole, but the hallway was quiet. Cautiously, I opened the door and poked my head out, looking both ways. The police officers were gone. They might be on another floor, or they left the building. "It's just bad luck or bad timing." I locked the door. "They weren't looking for you."

"Are you sure?"

"As sure as I can be." I pointed out the window. "This is far too elaborate a ploy for Scott to have concocted."

She nodded a few times, hugging her arms around her body. "Yeah, you're right."

"Do you want some tea?" I rummaged through the kitchen. If I didn't get caffeine inside of me soon, I'd hit the floor. I flexed my fingers against the residual tremor from the adrenaline dump. "Or a glass of water? Maybe a valium?"

She laughed, realizing the last was a joke. It might have been the first time I heard her laugh in amusement, not from nerves or sarcasm. "Is pushing pills your side hustle?"

"No, though I might consider it in the future." My mind circled back to today's appointments and contract negotiations. Opening the container of coffee pods, I put one in the brewer and shoved a mug beneath it. "Coffee?"

She shook her head. "That's the last thing I need." Dropping into a chair, she pulled her knees to her chest, looking down at the red marks on her hand from her own teeth. "I really thought he found me. You must think I'm crazy."

The machine let out a hiss, and I picked up the steaming mug. "No, but he might be." Pulling out the chair beside her, I sat down. "It turns out Scott's been unstable for a while now. Do you remember anything happening to him around the time he first hit you? Maybe someone died? His dad or someone at work?"

She stared at the light blue cup in my hand. "His dad passed before we got together. He mentioned it once, but I don't think he really cared. They weren't close."

"Do you know if he abused Scott?"

"I don't know. Is that why he's like this? I would think if you dealt with something like this as a kid, you'd never treat someone else like that since you know how terrible it is."

"I don't know. The statistics make it appear the chances are more likely, but you'd have to ask a psychologist."

Jade nodded. "Yeah, I know. One of my professors was a prison psychologist. She explained it, backed it by studies and everything, but I never understood."

"That's probably a good thing. It means you're normal."

She snorted. "I don't know what your life is like, Lucien, but this isn't normal."

"At least you recognize that." I smiled and sipped my coffee. She derailed my line of questioning, so I tried again. "What about other traumatic events in Scott's life?"

Jade thought for a while. "Something happened at work three years ago. I don't remember all the details, but Scott got called to a scene. I remember because we went to a funeral a week later. The responding officers had been killed."

"Did they catch the guy?"

"I thought they did, but," she chewed on her fingernail, "Scott moped around the house for a couple of weeks after that. Then he started drinking a lot more."

"Is that around the time he first hit you?"

She nodded.

"All right." I regretted my words, cringing. "It's not all right, but..."

"I know what you meant." She picked up my empty coffee cup and washed it in the sink. "Why does any of this matter?"

"Mr. Almeada wanted to know Scott's history. It might be relevant information he needs for the hearing."

From the silence that ensued, I knew Jade had reservations. But I didn't push. Almeada explained to her why this was important. Scott didn't leave her a choice. She needed to do something to keep him away, and unfortunately, a court order was the best our society had to remedy the situation.

"I should get back to the office." Glancing down at my sweat-stained and wrinkled shirt, I sighed. This time, I'd stop at home to shower and change. Apparently, I needed to keep a few sets of clothes in the office. Who knew private investigator work would require this much dry cleaning?

"Do you have to go?" She spun away from the sink, fear in her eyes.

"I can get you set up in another apartment or take you to a hotel if that would make you feel safer." Though hotels and motels would be some of the first places Scott would check after he finished searching the shelters and rescues.

"No, you've done enough." She swallowed. "Maybe I could come with you. I don't want to be alone right now."

"Let me call the office. Assuming Justin has everything under control, I can probably stick around for a little while and work from here."

"Yeah?"

"Yeah." This was a bad idea, but I was tired and stressed and didn't want any repeats of this morning. And since I knew Scott was desperate to find her, if Jade called a second time, I'd rush right over and break down the door, again.

FOURTEEN

"Lucien."

"Hmm?" I forced one eyelid to lift and then the other.

"It's morning. Do you have to go to work?"

"What?" I blinked and sat up. Empty takeout containers littered the coffee table. Grabbing my phone, I checked the time. 9AM. "Shit. I never sleep this late."

"Thanks for staying." Jade popped another pod into the coffeemaker and pressed the button. "Do you want some coffee?"

"Yes, thanks." I rubbed a hand through my hair and stumbled to the bathroom. I spent the entire day working from Jade's couch since the incident with the police left her rattled. Admittedly, it rattled me too, though I wasn't entirely sure why. But I could see it on my face. I looked like hell. Two days without a shower or shave left me ripe and looking a little bit homeless.

Yesterday afternoon, Justin brought the signed contracts over. Cross Security signed twelve of the fourteen candidates I selected, which was two more than I thought we'd get and four more than we needed. Unfortunately, they didn't start until Monday, and I didn't know any of the security specialists well enough to trust them to watch

Jade, who was leery of everyone, even me.

She kept her distance from Justin when he brought the files and then returned with the takeout. He and I went over the day's details and meetings while eating Chinese and sitting on the couch. But even though I came rushing to her rescue, Jade kept her distance, even circling around to avoid walking near us. I couldn't thrust an unknown bodyguard on her, unless she'd be more comfortable with one of the two women I hired. That was a possibility we'd have to discuss at a future date.

I stepped out of the bathroom. "Did Justin offend you?"

"No, he's been great."

I picked up the mug and took a sip. Testing out my theory, I reached for the milk beside her hand, and she withdrew. "That bastard, Scott, really did a number on you."

She met my eyes but didn't respond. We stood in the kitchen, drinking coffee in silence. I had too much to do. I shouldn't have slept on the couch. I could barely believe I fell asleep or slept as long as I did. Gulping down the rest, I put my mug in the sink.

"I'll see about getting the bedroom and bathroom doors fixed." Though I'd have to be careful if I sourced out the work. It looked like someone broke in, and that would draw undue attention. The last thing any of us wanted were more cops snooping around. "Are you okay?"

"Yes."

"Okay." I grabbed my jacket off the hanger and slipped it on to conceal my holster. "I'll see you later."

After showering, I felt better. More human. So I went to the office. My receptionist had the weekends off, but Justin was hard at work. He was a godsend, the only bright light from my time on Wall Street. He'd been an intern, my intern. When I suspected my boss of embezzling, Justin helped me get access to the files. The SEC didn't know about his involvement. He could have stayed and become a trader or investment banker or whatever it was he originally intended. But people talk. Rumors spread, and even though no one had any proof he helped me, they suspected it and blackballed him too. So I owed him. And after these last few days, I really owed him.

"Do you think she's safe?" he asked, not looking up from the computer screen.

"As safe as she can be."

"Even with the police sniffing around?"

I slapped a copy of today's paper on his desk. The ATM robbery got a tiny photo beneath the fold. "The reason for their lurking looks legit. It was just bad timing."

"Do you want to move her somewhere else? I found a few alternative locations."

"Maybe after the court proceedings. It'll depend on how things play out." I went into my office. "Right now, we have more pressing matters." And I couldn't keep shelling out cash.

Opening my presentation files, I reviewed the details about my perspective clients and tailored each presentation to fit their needs. I needed paying customers before I bankrupted my personal savings while trying to get things off the ground. Signing a big name would solve most of my problems. Once I had a steady income stream, I could hire men like Amir Karam and expand. The first thing I'd do would be move out of this office. Image was everything, and this place wouldn't impress a cockroach.

When I locked down each of my four presentations, I reread the jackets on my new hires. My twelve new employees would report to work Monday morning. Thankfully, I already had an employee handbook and crisis manual ready to go. I even paid a few thousand to have a set of training videos prepared, and I hired a retired Secret Service agent to conduct the training sessions and set up a few obstacle courses and drills. But I hoped this would be nothing more than a refresher course for them. Bodyguard work required a particular skill set, which they already possessed but with a few tweaks. Six of the men had previous experience in private security and came highly recommended. Everything should run smoothly, though I never expected anything to ever run smoothly.

By the time I finished getting everything set up, it was dark. Justin left three hours ago. It was time I did the same. Before heading home, I stopped by the hardware store, picked up some supplies to fix the doors, and headed to Jade's.

Last night, she stayed in the bedroom while Justin and I worked in the living room. Tonight, she stayed in the living room while I worked in the bedroom. After replacing the doorknob with a new one that had a much better lock, I hammered in the loose parts of the doorframe. Hopefully, the landlord wouldn't pay too much attention since I hoped to get my security deposit back.

The bathroom was easier to fix since the doorjamb remained intact. The lock on that door was so cheap, the internal mechanism gave out under the pressure, so I replaced that doorknob too. Wiping my hands on a towel, I glanced around. Jade hadn't unpacked anything. The only items on the counter were things I ordered for the apartment.

"Do you need anything else?" I asked.

Jade looked up from her copy of *People* magazine. "No." But I saw the fear in her eyes.

I took a step back, dropping the hammer and screwdriver into the plastic bag. Once they were out of sight, she visibly relaxed. The only thought in my head was Scott Renwin was a piece of shit. The police department knew it, but they didn't do a damn thing about it. And tonight, I'd find out why.

FIFTEEN

"Hey. You aren't supposed to be in here," the officer said.

I turned, automatically lifting my hands to waist height so he'd know I wasn't armed. Slowly, I removed the flashlight from my mouth. "You're right."

"Let's go, buddy." He jerked his chin toward the door. "How did you get in here?"

I chuckled, stepping away from the dark shelves and into the light. "It wasn't too hard." I recognized him, though I didn't recall his name.

"You're—"

"Yep." I cleared my throat, the lie already prepared. "My father said he had some files and records pulled for me, but when I checked his office, they weren't there. Someone forgot to do it. I thought I'd just grab them myself since I didn't want to make a fuss and get anyone in trouble." I stepped closer, compliant and friendly. "I guess we better call him and get this straightened out."

The officer didn't like that idea. "Maybe I can help you find them. It's late. We don't need to inconvenience him."

I held the smile, though my thoughts went dark. I doubted anything could inconvenience him more than my existence. "Are you sure?"

"No problem. What are you looking for?"

So I told him. If the officer was suspicious why I needed access to Sgt. Renwin's case files and evaluations from three years ago, he didn't act like it. Instead, he went to the terminal in the corner and typed in the request. Unfortunately, the files weren't digitized. I already looked.

"You know," I said as he went in search of the box on the shelf, "I helped design that system." I jerked my chin at the computer. It was a few years ago, right after I graduated college but before signing up for the police academy, back when I thought being a cop was the greatest thing in the world. A lot had changed, but the backdoor I created into the system had not. Though it hadn't helped me access any of the information I needed on Scott since performance reports and evaluations weren't stored digitally.

"How old were you?" The officer reached for a box beside the one I had been searching. "You must have been a kid."

I laughed. "Thanks, but I'm not that much of a prodigy." Spotting the department psychologist's notes in the box I had abandoned, I kept my eyes on the officer's back while I carefully reached inside and slipped the notes into my jacket pocket without him noticing.

"And your father still has you running errands for us?" The officer pulled out a few files and handed them to me. "He should put you on the payroll."

"Who says I'm not?" I teased, though I had to work hard to keep my fists from clenching and my jaw from tightening. I stared down at the files until I was sure my poker face was back in place. "Seems light." I hefted the stack.

"We didn't have much to go on from that incident." He glanced down. "The Sarge caught a tough break with that one. Is this for a commendation or something?"

"Yeah, but keep it quiet."

"Will do."

Instead of taking the files and signing them out, I said I just needed to verify a few details, and when the officer wasn't looking, I snapped photos of each of the pages, returned the files to the box, and left without another word. That could have gone better, but I wasn't in cuffs. So I shouldn't complain.

Safely inside my car, I checked the GPS tracker to make sure Scott was home, then I drove to Jade's, pushed my seat back, and spread the shrink's file out on the dashboard. I had work to do. I just didn't know where to begin.

The incident, as the officer referred to it, occurred over three years ago. A liquor store hold-up went south. The owner and two customers were shot and killed. Sgt. Renwin arrived first on scene. According to the report, he was inside the store when a second unit arrived. Shots were fired, killing a rookie officer and his T.O. Renwin failed to notice the shooter had ducked down a nearby alleyway to count his score.

Renwin chased the suspect and apprehended him two blocks from the original scene. But the suspect had tossed the gun somewhere along the way. And the sergeant didn't notice when this happened and failed to mention it in his report. When the weapon was recovered, the police couldn't positively link it back to the shooter. The DA's office rushed the case through since two cops and three civilians had been slain, but the grand jury failed to indict. Once released, the shooter committed a home invasion, killing a tender age child before being brought down by responding officers.

Even though the department didn't find Renwin at fault for the officers' deaths, he was required to attend mandated counseling sessions. This was the tipping point, the traumatic incident, the thing that turned the man into a monster. But the shrink signed off, saying Renwin was fit to return to active duty.

However, after the home invasion, Renwin became violent and belligerent, blaming himself for the child's death. His commanding officer suggested anger management, but Renwin refused. No matter how hard he denied it, deep down, Renwin knew the truth. He was angry at himself and the world. Instead of finding a healthy outlet, he drank more and more. And one day that wasn't enough. So he started knocking around the dirtbags he arrested. But it still wasn't enough. Eventually, he turned that internal hatred outward and focused it on the one person who loved him – Jade.

I dropped the file to the seat and stared out the windshield, a little nauseous and unsettled by the revelation. Maybe I was wrong. Maybe Renwin just liked to beat up the weak as indicated by his perceived inferiority complex. Either way, I found the one helpful piece of information I hoped we'd find. His commanding officer wrote a note in Renwin's file indicating the sergeant refused to go to anger management. That meant the department knew Renwin had a problem and was a ticking time bomb. It might not be proof that Renwin hit Jade, but it came pretty damn close. It would be enough. Almeada would take that one fact and build a rock solid case.

SIXTEEN

I kept sneaking quick peeks at my watch. The hearing should be underway. Did Scott Renwin show up in person? Did he have counsel? Toying with my phone, I checked the tracker's location. According to this, Scott's truck was parked at the precinct. Maybe he couldn't get the day off, or maybe he drove a cruiser to court. The bastard might have shown up in full police regalia in the hopes of swaying the judge's opinion. I wouldn't put it past him.

"Mr. Cross?"

I blinked and clicked to another slide. "As I was saying, data breaches could have catastrophic repercussions." Luckily, my carefully crafted notes and detailed presentation got my mind back on track. I didn't even finish going through the slides before my first official Cross Security client signed the contract.

"I don't need to see anything else. Your investments and tips made me millions. I trust you. If you say this is what needs to be done to safeguard my company and assets, I say let's do it."

"Okay, great. My assistant will schedule the initial review and consultation, and we'll take it from there."

We shook hands, concluding my second meeting of the

day. The first one didn't go nearly as well. My potential client wanted to review the information and present it to his partners before signing the contract. Still, I got the impression it was a strong maybe and not an overt no.

After my second appointment left, Justin stepped into my office. "We got one. Is it too early to start celebrating?" He held up a bottle of scotch.

"No, but I better not come back from lunch to find you sloshed. Don't forget our final appointment is this afternoon with Miranda." I straightened my tie and buttoned my jacket. "Did you order a car?"

"Yes. It's waiting downstairs."

"Excellent." I dug the phone out of my pocket, but I didn't have any messages. "Hold down the fort while I'm gone."

"Yes, sir."

"And save me a glass of scotch."

"Will do."

I slipped inside the town car, glad to have a few moments of quiet before we picked up Mr. Rathbone on our way to the restaurant. I needed the time to rehearse my next presentation. Since Rathbone had an army of private security and a trusted board who kept his company up-to-date with the times, he didn't want Cross Security to pitch him new ideas or protections. He wanted me to evaluate his security measures and personnel, find weaknesses, and eliminate them. Despite his grandfatherly exterior, Rathbone was the most cutthroat and ruthless man I'd ever met. And he wanted me to excise any malignancies with precision and ease.

The car picked him up outside his office skyscraper. Maybe I should have gotten a limo instead of a town car, but the idea seemed too ostentatious at the time. Now, I wasn't sure. We made small talk until we arrived at the restaurant. Once there, Rathbone ordered a steak, bloody, and a bottle of red wine. I followed suit, launching into my pitch while he sliced through the meat with zeal.

Around our second bottle of wine, Rathbone and I reached a gentlemen's agreement, shaking on the deal. His legal department would review the contract. If they required any amendments, they'd reach out to my legal department, which at the moment was Mr. Almeada, and let him know. Cross Security had arrived.

We finished the bottle, and the car took Rathbone back to his office before dropping me off at mine. I tipped the driver more than I should on account of my good fortune. Rathbone wanted background checks on every employee, and he employed thousands. Working for him could keep us afloat for months, even if no other clients came in, but I knew they would. This was just the beginning.

My afternoon appointment showed up a half hour early, surprising me. Miranda didn't want to listen to my presentation. She was looking for a security detail to accompany her while touring. After checking the dates to make sure my new hires had ample time to complete training, I told her it wouldn't be a problem, and she signed on the dotted line.

"What about your manager and the studio?" I asked. "Don't they usually hire the help?"

She laughed. "Obviously, you haven't been following my career or the shakeup in the music biz."

"Sorry, I've been a little busy."

She eyed me up and down. "I'll bet."

"Come on, Miranda." When I first struck gold, my boss brought me in to assist on diversifying Miranda's portfolio, but she'd taken a liking to me and made it clear I was the only one who could handle her assets. "You know how much work I've put into this."

"I do. Why do you think I took this meeting?"

"You missed me."

"That too." She held out her hand, and I brought it to my lips. "You know I can make room on the tour for one more. I'd let you coordinate my security any day."

"But who would run all this? I can't just dump it in Justin's lap."

"Sure, you could." She leaned across my desk and brushed her lips against my cheek. "Just think about it."

"Absolutely."

She gave me a cockeyed look and sashayed out of the office, blowing a kiss to Justin, and telling my receptionist to keep an eye on the two of us men. I dropped into my chair, elated.

Opening my spreadsheet, I updated the projections. Perhaps we'd actually get into the black by our second quarter. As soon as that happened, I could start expanding. More employees, additional advertising, updated services. The possibilities left me giddy, or it was the heady mix of perfectly aged wine, Miranda's intoxicating perfume, and the dollar signs dancing in front of my eyes.

The outer office door opened, and for a moment, I wondered if Miranda had forgotten something. But I didn't hear her gentle lilt. Instead, I heard a deep, raspy voice.

"Take a seat. I'll see if he's busy." My receptionist knocked on my door before stepping inside. "Mr. Cross, we have a walk-in. Do you want me to ask him to make an appointment?"

"No, that's okay. Send him in."

"Yes, sir." She exited, leaving the door open. "Right through there."

I closed my spreadsheet and stuck Miranda's contract inside my drawer. I already signed three new clients. Maybe this would be lucky number four. But I was dead wrong. It took every ounce of self-control to keep the impassive, professional look on my face.

"Mr. Cross," he extended his hand, and I stood to shake it, "I'm looking for my girlfriend. She's gone missing. I was hoping you could help me find her."

SEVENTEEN

"How long has she been missing?" I asked, playing along. "Have you spoken to the police?"

"They can't help me." Scott sat back in the chair; his expression unreadable.

I thought I had him pegged the first time I laid eyes on him. He wore his emotions on his sleeve, but now he was calm. Too calm. I searched his eyes for a moment before busying myself with checking my drawers for a pad of paper. He must have taken something in order to keep calm and sedate.

"Tell me about her, mister..." I waited. Two could play at this game.

"Biggs. Leonard Biggs."

I nodded, wondering why he used a fake name. Could this be a coincidence? Did Scott Renwin have a doppelganger? My gut said no. Scott stared at me, squinting for a moment before rubbing his eyes. Did he recognize me from our brief encounter in the airport parking garage? It didn't matter. He knew who I was. That's why he came here. He knew I stashed Jade somewhere. And he intended to find out where.

"Tell me about her. What's her name? When did she go

missing?"

He pulled a photograph of Jade out of his pocket and placed it on my desk. He remained focused entirely on me. "Jade McNamara. She left about a week ago."

I lifted the photo and leaned back in my chair, aware of the weight of his stare. "Left?" I put the photo down and met his eyes. Ice ran through my veins. I wouldn't give anything away, not to a prick like him.

"A family member fell ill."

"So you know where she is." My brows knit together. "What's the problem?"

"It's a lie." The anger ignited in his eyes and coursed through his body, but he swallowed it away. "She doesn't have an Aunt Bonnie."

"Huh?" I steepled my fingers and tapped them against my chin. "Have you spoken to her? Maybe you misheard what she said. Bad connection."

"We haven't spoken. I found a note in our apartment. Her things were gone. She won't answer her phone. I tried calling several times, but nothing. She just disappeared."

"Do you suspect foul play?"

Something disconcerting flickered in his eyes. "Yes."

"In that case, you need to contact the police or FBI."

"I don't think any of us wants that." He let the threat hang in the air. "Missing persons cases can be tough to crack. The police have hundreds, maybe thousands, to solve. They don't have time for this. *I* don't have time for this. That's why I thought hiring a private investigator would be better. Faster. More to the point."

"I hate to say it, but you've come to the wrong place. I'm not much of a private investigator. I specialize in corporate security."

"Oh." Scott didn't move or budge. He just stared with those fiery eyes. "Are you sure you won't make an exception? I'm prepared to pay whatever you want."

I didn't like this game. Scott knew I was involved in Jade's disappearance. I didn't know how, but he did. And he concocted this tale to find out where I stashed her. Maybe he thought he could buy me off. "What do you do for a living, Mr. Biggs?"

"Why does that matter?"

"I was just wondering how much you're willing to pay to get her back."

He stared at me, a cross between smug self-assuredness and a burning desire to break every bone in my body. "I'll do whatever it takes."

That answer worried me. "Do you think someone abducted Ms. McNamara?" I wasn't sure what other private investigators would say under these circumstances, but I didn't think many of them would be stupid enough to find themselves in this situation. Still, kidnapping made a lot of sense based on the bullshit Scott spewed. Though, I'd just seen *Taken*, so that might have had something to do with it. "If you're reasonably well off, this could be a ransom situation. Once again, I urge you to go to the authorities."

Scott laughed bitterly. "Are you for real?"

As real as you are. "Like I said, I deal with corporate clients. Kidnapping and ransoms are commonplace in their world." I narrowed my eyes. "But probably not in yours."

"No."

"What do you do for a living?" I tried again, hoping to confuse Scott into thinking I was too clueless to be involved. Unfortunately, he wasn't as stupid as he looked.

Scott thought for a moment. "I work construction."

Nice, I thought, *that would explain the truck.* "So it's not a kidnapping and ransom. But you still think she was taken against her will?" I picked up the photograph of Jade, fighting to maintain the cold detachment as the ice in my veins melted and boiled.

"I just want to find her. I have to find her. She gets confused. She doesn't realize she needs me to take care of her."

I picked up my pen. "Does she have any diagnosed medical or psychological conditions?"

"No, but..."

"But what?"

"She can't take care of herself."

"Why not?"

"She just can't."

I wrote Jade's name on the first line and put the alias Scott gave me in the top corner of the pad, just for something to do. "That sounds like a difficult burden to bear. Are you sure you want to keep doing this?"

"Of course. I love her."

I stopped writing and stared at him. "Be honest, Mr. Biggs. Do you think something happened to her? Or do you think she left you?"

He glared at me; whatever sedative he took wasn't enough to completely extinguish the rage. "The only reason she'd ever leave me is if someone talked her into it." And Scott knew he was staring at that someone.

But I remained cool. "Any idea who's responsible?"

"No, but I intend to find out." He watched me closely. "And when I do, that person's going to pay." We stared at one another warily. He knew. I knew. But he didn't break from the charade. "I'm prepared to do this with or without your help, but I imagine things will work out better for all of us with your help."

Finally, I broke eye contact, painting a pleasant, business smile on my face. "All right. Sure. Tell me about Jade. Where does she work? I need a list of friends. Family. Anyone you believe she might confide in. Her phone number. E-mail address. Whatever contact information you might have." I slid the paper and pen across the desk. "While you fill that out, let me grab a contract. It's five hundred dollars a day, plus expenses. Will that be a problem?"

He dropped the pen onto the desk. "Let's cut to the chase. Why don't you give me a nice round figure instead?"

"Sorry, I don't know how long it'll take to locate her. And results aren't guaranteed."

He stood, his fists clenched, the veins bulging in his wrists and forearms. Maybe he'd hit me, and we'd put this entire thing to rest right now. But he didn't. "Just think about it, and let me know when you change your mind." He placed something on the pad of paper and left the office.

I looked down, recognizing the GPS tracker I'd left on his rear bumper. Shit.

EIGHTEEN

"Justin, call the exterminator, tell him I need the office swept for bugs."

My assistant looked up, knowing not to question me. "Okay."

I turned to the receptionist. "We might have bed bugs. I thought I saw one crawling around near the baseboards, so until we know for sure, you might as well stay home. I'll let you know once the office has been cleared. And thank you for doing such a wonderful job today."

She gave me an odd look. "Sir?"

"Go on." I nodded at the door. "And if anyone bothers you, let me know."

She knew something odd happened but didn't question me. After collecting her belongings and wishing us a good night, she left the office.

Every fiber in my body said I had to check on Jade, but that's what Scott would expect. So I didn't make any calls or leave work. Since he found the tracker I planted and left it in my office, there was no question he was on to me. And without being able to monitor his movements, I'd have to take extra precautions. How did he find the tracker and discover my connection to Jade? It didn't make sense.

Thirty minutes later, the exterminator, an IT expert who specialized in locating surveillance equipment, checked my office. He didn't find anything, but to be on the safe side, he and Justin checked our servers and network to make sure there hadn't been any data breaches. We were clear. Scott wasn't an evil genius. He was just angry, which made him dangerous.

"Phones are clear too," the exterminator said.

"Thanks." But I didn't risk making a call. The police could tap the line. I'd have to get a burner. Actually, we should probably keep some of those stocked at the office. I added it to my list of things to consider in the future.

Scott Renwin had turned my fledgling business on its head, and I didn't like it. He'd regret it. I'd make sure of it.

"Boss," my assistant said, worry etching his boyish features, "who was that guy?"

"That's the bastard Jade ran away from."

"And he came here to ask for your help?"

"He came to threaten me." I blew out a breath. "Look, I need you to keep on top of our new hires. Do a little digging, and make sure Scott didn't reach out to any of them. I doubt he did, but it doesn't hurt to make sure. After that, monitor their training. Keep me updated on how that goes. And steer clear of the office until this blows over. Do what you can from home, and watch out for tails or anything suspicious. You see anything, especially a ridiculously oversized truck, report it."

"But he's a cop."

"It doesn't matter. You work for me. The police will keep you safe, even from one of their own."

Ignoring the questioning look on Justin's face, I grabbed my gun and credentials from my desk drawer, along with the freshly signed contracts, and rode the elevator to the lobby. A police cruiser remained parked on the other side of the street. Renwin was a piece of work, but he'd learn I wasn't a defenseless schmuck he could intimidate or push around. Since he wanted to wage war, I'd bring the war to him.

I didn't go to my car. Instead, I walked a few blocks to the nearest subway station and descended the stairs. While

I waited on the platform, I caught sight of Scott in my periphery, doing his best to remain hidden behind a pillar.

When the train arrived, I entered the open doors and headed toward the other end of the car. As soon as I glimpsed Scott enter, I found a spot to stand near the back, next to a second set of doors, and waited for the telltale chime alerting passengers the doors were closing. Then I darted out, turning to see Scott stuck inside the sealed train car.

Since he found the tracker I planted, I feared he might have reciprocated, so I left my car parked outside the office and took a cab to Reeves and Almeada. I had a million questions. Mr. Almeada better be able to answer them.

"Mr. Cross?" the secretary put down the phone.

"I need to see him. Now." I didn't even slow as I moved past her desk toward Almeada's corner office.

"Wait." She hurried after me, her heels clicking frantically against the tile floor.

I pulled open Almeada's door. Thankfully, the attorney wasn't in a meeting with a client. "We need to talk. What the hell happened today?"

Almeada looked up at the sudden interruption. His gaze came to rest on the frazzled woman behind me. He flicked his wrist, giving her a slight headshake, and she disappeared. "What's wrong, Cross? Have you spoken to Jade?"

Jade, shit. "I need to use your phone."

"What?"

"Your phone." I moved to the desk and picked up the receiver, checking for a dial tone before I punched in Jade's number. "I have to pick up a throwaway, but until then, I just need a few minutes. I have to make sure she's okay."

"Jade?"

My gaze shot to his face. "Who else?"

"Hello?" Jade's voice filled me with relief.

"Hi, it's me. It's Lucien. I just wanted to check on you. Are you at the apartment?"

"Yes."

"Okay, good. Stay there. Keep the doors locked. I'll be by soon."

"What's wrong? What's going on?" she asked.

"Nothing. Everything's fine. We'll discuss what happened in court today and work on devising our next steps, okay? Just stay put."

"Yeah, okay," she replied, bewildered.

I hung up, taking my first full breath since Renwin walked into my office.

Almeada poured a drink and placed the glass on the desk beside me. "Sit down and tell me what's going on."

So I did. "He's on to me. I don't know how."

Almeada snorted. "Take your pick. He could have made you at the airport, or someone at the precinct said something to the wrong person, or Jade looked you up on Scott's computer."

"She said she didn't."

"Clients aren't always completely honest."

"It doesn't matter. What matters is Scott knows. What happened in court?"

"Mr. Renwin denied the claims. He showed up, calm and rational. He spoke eloquently. He was polite to Jade. He didn't do anything the judge would construe as threatening. He didn't try to approach her, argue with her, or do any of the things most people in his situation do. She came off emotional and unstable. He looked like a fucking boy scout."

"A stoned boy scout."

Almeada shrugged. "It doesn't matter. The judge listened to Ms. McNamara's story and erred on the side of caution. I didn't present any of the evidence we obtained. I don't want the other side to get wind of what we have in the event we need to use it to get a permanent restraining order."

"Smart thinking. We'll probably need it. Scott's angry, and it'll only get worse once the police department receives official notice. Jade can't stay in that apartment. Scott knows I helped her. He'll use that information to track her down." I scowled. "He wants to use me to find her. That's why he stopped by the office. He thought he could bribe me, and when that didn't work, he figured he'd intimidate me and I'd take him right to her."

"It's a good thing he underestimated you. I can arrange for temporary housing while you figure this out."

"Good."

Almeada picked up the phone and made a few calls. My thoughts drifted to Sara and the officer guarding the records room. I didn't think Sara would betray me, but who knows what she might have said if someone questioned why she was digging through Renwin's files. And the officer in the records room easily could have run his mouth. Then again, the waitress or bartender at KC's might have tipped off Scott. This wasn't good. I already bumbled my first private investigator gig, and now I had to figure out how to get it back on track. I promised Jade I'd keep her safe, and I was a man of my word. I just had to find a way to keep my promise.

NINETEEN

"Lucien, I don't understand. Why do I have to leave? What's going on?"

"It's just a precaution. Mr. Almeada and I want to keep you safe."

She stared into my eyes. "Scott knows. He found me."

"No."

"Don't lie to me."

"I'm not."

Searching my face for answers, she said, "I know that look. I'm used to seeing it staring back at me in the mirror. What did he do? I know he did something. How bad is it?"

Suddenly parched, I licked my lips and cleared my throat. "He found the tracker I placed on his truck and came to my office to return it."

"Does he know where I am?"

I shook my head and peered out the window. "Not yet. That's why we need to move you."

Her eyes grew even wider. "What's he going to do to you?"

"He can't do anything to me. Don't worry. I just want to keep you safe. Since the apartment is registered under one of my LLCs, there's a small chance he could discover it if he digs deep enough. So we'll move you before that happens. Reeves and Almeada keep a few apartments in the city for their out-of-town clients. They're much nicer than this dump. You'll be safe there."

She looked around the barely furnished apartment. "Okay."

It didn't take Jade long to pack her things. When she was done, I went outside and hailed a cab. After helping the cabbie load her luggage into the car, I paid him and gave him her new address.

"You're not coming?" she asked.

"No, I have some things to take care of. Mr. Almeada will meet you at the apartment and help you get settled. You have my new number should anything arise."

She nodded, though I could see she wanted to argue. "You better call me tomorrow."

I grinned. "When did you get so bossy?"

"I'm serious."

"Okay." I opened the car door and waited for her to slide inside. "I'll talk to you tomorrow." Shutting the door, I tapped on the side of the cab and stared at the rental car. That was another waste. But I could use it in the interim, while my car remained at the office.

I trudged up the stairs and let myself back inside. Then I cleaned the apartment, so no one would ever know Jade had been here. Unfortunately, I couldn't erase the memories of the two police officers who had knocked on the door the other morning, but they never got her name. So I didn't concern myself too much with that aspect of damage control.

When I finished, I went to the nearest electronics store and stocked up on the basics. It took a couple of hours to jerry-rig the security system with the sensors and pinhole cameras I bought. After checking to make sure the wireless signal was strong and the footage was automatically backed up to my cloud drive, I left the apartment. If anyone dropped by the apartment, I would know about it.

Should Scott discover this apartment, he'd stop by, just like my office and the rest of the properties I rented or owned. He knew I had her, and he'd do anything to get her back. In the event he came after Jade, I wanted proof to bury him.

On my way home, I couldn't help but notice every police car on the road. Call it paranoia or healthy observation, but until now, patrol cars had never made me nervous. Now they did. Shake it off, Cross. The last thing I needed was Scott Renwin getting in my head.

I parked in my normal space and greeted the doorman. "Anything going on I should know about?"

"No, sir."

"Okay." I reached into my pocket, palming a few bills before extending my hand. We shook. "Should the police show up, I'd appreciate advanced notice."

He grinned, tucking the money into his pocket without looking at it. "Now what have you done, Mr. Cross? Are you a wanted man?"

"Do you think I'd tell you if I was?" I grinned. "I'll leave the details up to your imagination."

"Very good, sir."

As soon as I stepped foot inside my apartment, I checked my security system. No one had entered or lurked in the hallways outside my door, not that I believed Scott could gain access to my building with anything less than a valid warrant, but I didn't intend to underestimate him. He found the tracker, and he'd been smart enough to sedate himself for court. Clearly, he wasn't stupid or as stupid as his face led me to believe.

Even though my apartment and the one I rented for Jade remained secure, I had trouble sleeping that night. The conversation with Scott played on a loop in my head. Did he honestly think I'd give Jade up for a few bucks? Idly, I wondered what he planned to do when she went back to work. Based on our conversation, he seemed determined to violate the terms of the TRO the first chance he got, but Mr. Almeada believed that might be a knee-jerk reaction to the proceedings. Most people wanted to confront their accusers and, in the case of domestic abuse, knock some sense into them as well. The thought sickened me. Maybe tomorrow would be better. But I was wrong.

TWENTY

When I left my apartment the next morning, a cruiser pulled behind me. It didn't flash its lights or siren, and even when I switched lanes to let it pass, it stayed behind me. It stayed on me all the way to the coffee shop.

I stopped at the café I frequented most mornings, expecting the patrolman to follow me inside. But he didn't. At least not right away. I ordered my usual and paid for a second cappuccino with extra foam. "That's not for me," I said. "But when that cop comes in here, tell him Mr. Cross treated him to a cup." I picked up the paper cup that would hold his drink and the marker and wrote on it, *Blow me.* Then I over-tipped the barista, bought a paper, and took a seat in the back.

Ten minutes later, when I didn't come out, the cop came in. It wasn't Scott, just some patrolman he ordered to follow me. The poor guy was just another pawn the sergeant used for his own twisted purposes. He should report his boss for abuse of power, and if he didn't, I would.

By the time the cop made his way to the front of the line, the cappuccino was waiting for him. He turned in my direction, and I lifted my own cup, smirking. He read what I wrote on his coffee and glared at me. I raised a suggestive eyebrow, but the patrolman didn't engage. Instead, he went out to his car and drove away.

An hour later, I finished my coffee and the crossword puzzle and headed to the office. Since I told everyone to stay away, it didn't matter what time I showed up. Justin had already sent me a dozen texts concerning our new hires, our new clients, and some messages Almeada's office had left him. Today would be another busy day.

When I arrived, I noticed my car didn't look quite right. Parking near it, I got out to find all four of my tires slashed. Cursing, I looked up, searching for nearby security cameras. Unfortunately, the attack didn't set off my car alarm or it'd still be beeping, which meant it was unlikely someone noticed who had done this. But I knew who was responsible. I just didn't have proof.

Pissed, I entered the office building, spoke to building security, requested they check their footage to see if anything was caught on camera, and took the elevator up. As soon as I let myself into the office, I picked up the phone and called the police. They assured me someone was on their way. While I waited, I phoned Almeada and updated him on the situation.

"Can you prove it was Renwin?"

"I doubt it." Unless building security performed a miracle.

"Okay. In that case, you might want to restrain yourself from pointing fingers until you have proof."

"How's Jade settling in?"

"She's fine. I'm hoping to get her back to work in a couple of days. Since Renwin's this unbalanced, I'll have the paperwork ready ahead of time in case we need to request an emergency hearing."

"If it comes down to that, I want the bastard behind bars." I looked out the window, spotting a police cruiser pulling to a stop in front of my building. "Right now, I have to make a report."

"Do you want me to stop by?"

"I can handle it."

"Are you sure?" Almeada asked.

"Well, if I can't, I'll call you from lockup."

Sgt. Scott Renwin stood beside his cruiser. I approached him, doing my best to feign surprise. But I doubted even a world-class actor could successfully pull off that feat.

"You're a cop? I thought you worked construction." I narrowed my eyes at the nametag tacked to his left breast. "Sgt. S. Renwin. Didn't you say your name was Leonard Biggs?"

"Sir, we've never met." Hatred poured from his eyes.

"What's the S stand for? Shithead?"

Scott pulled a flashlight from his belt and shone it directly in my eyes, which was an asshole move, probably revenge for the shithead comment. "Have you ingested any illegal substances? Maybe you've been drinking?"

I glared at him. "Sorry, you must just have one of those faces. You look like this crazy bastard I met yesterday. The kind of scumbag who puts hands on a woman to make himself feel more like a man. You know, just a nobody asshole who thinks he can push people around and threaten them into doing whatever he wants."

"Oh, so you think you're a tough guy, Mr. Cross?"

"How do you know my name, if we haven't met?"

"From the phone call you placed."

"Right." I continued to glare at him as he returned the flashlight to its rightful place on his belt.

"What seems to be the problem? I received a call about property damage."

I pointed to my car. "I found it like that this morning."

"Where were you when this happened?"

"Wouldn't you like to know?"

Scott squeezed the pen in his hand so hard it bent in half. Exhaling slowly, he crossed the street to inspect the damage. He was on edge, ready to snap just like the pen. I wanted to push him. It was daylight. With dozens of people around, one of them would pull out a phone and record an act of police brutality. As a rule, most people hated cops.

I jogged after him. "Do you know what they say about men who stab things? They're compensating for their inability to perform in the bedroom."

"You should watch yourself, Mr. Cross. It looks like someone *blew* your tires."

"Lucky for me, that's not the first time I've been blown today."

Scott clenched his fists and stood. *C'mon, hit me,* I thought. His chest heaved, and he pressed himself against me. I stared expectantly at him. Waiting. Hoping. An arrogant grin plastered across my face. If I were him, I'd hit me. After ten seconds, Scott stepped back, focusing on taking down a proper account of the damage.

I placed a forearm against the roof of the car and leaned in. "Let me make one thing clear. I won't let you lay a hand on her again. You can't scare me, so back off. And let her go. You still have a career. You can have a life. Just leave her alone."

Renwin stood up straight and shoved me against the car. "Is that what she told you? Because it's a lie. I never hurt her."

"The bruises on her body say otherwise." I looked down at his hands still pressed against my chest. "For someone who claims he isn't violent, your actions make that hard to believe."

"Tell me where she is, or a few blown tires will be the least of your problems."

"Sorry, that's privileged information."

"I could arrest you."

"On what grounds?" Despite my baser instincts, I didn't struggle or fight back. I had yet to lay a hand on Scott. Unfortunately, the bastard was smart enough to leave his bodycam off. And while suspicious and possibly a violation of police regulations, it wouldn't prove any claims I made.

"Stalking."

"Go ahead."

Scott shoved me harder into the car and stepped back. He scribbled down the basis for the call and held it out for me to sign. I took the misshapen pen, signed the bottom, and grabbed the copy he thrust against my chest. "You have a good day. It might very well be your last," he warned.

TWENTY-ONE

I sat at my desk, steaming, as I planned a counterstrike. First things first. I had to figure out how Scott discovered Jade had come to me for help. The tracker didn't link back to me, and after making a few calls to some friends at the precinct, I knew he hadn't called in any favors to have the transmitted location traced. Sara swore she didn't say a word. She also urged me to call my father.

"Daddy dearest has more important things to worry about," I said.

"Lucien, stop being so damn stubborn. Do you have any idea the kind of hell that'll rain down on you? Renwin is a sergeant. He could send a dozen uniforms to ruin your day."

"In that case, I'd like to file a formal complaint."

"Lucien," she sighed, exasperated.

"No, I'm serious."

She mumbled something I couldn't hear. "You'll have to come here to fill out the paperwork."

"Great. I'll stop by when I finish work for the day."

"Fine, but think about calling your father. If you don't, maybe I will."

"He won't help me. He never does. He made his choice a

long time ago." Hanging up, I brought up the list of names of people who'd filed complaints against Sgt. Renwin.

Justin had already contacted several of them. They all had similar stories. Scott bullied them, illegally searched their person or vehicle, and used excessive force. Unfortunately, most of them had records for distributing narcotics or engaging in prostitution, which lessened their complaints in the eyes of the police department. The few who didn't failed to follow up or were told the matter was being investigated.

So I'd take a different approach. Maybe I'd go straight to IA. Scott was belligerent and unprofessional. Belligerent, that's one word that popped up repeatedly in his fitness reports and complaints. It fit. I should check the dictionary to see if his photo was next to the definition. While I drafted what I wanted to say, a man entered the outer office.

"Knock, knock," Almeada called. "Anyone here?"

"In my office." I glanced up as he entered. "How'd you get inside?"

He cocked an eyebrow. "Door was open."

For a moment, I forgot I told my receptionist to take some time off. "Right." I pushed away from the desk and rubbed my eyes. "I don't think Scott will back off. I told him he needs to leave Jade alone. That this has to stop."

"And?"

"I'm pretty sure he threatened to kill me."

"Did you get it on tape?"

"No."

"Witnesses?"

I shook my head.

"Did you threaten him first?"

"Not really."

Almeada went to the bar in the corner of my office and poured a drink, even though it was barely lunchtime. "Cross, I understand this thing," he waved his hand around the room, "is new to you. So let me tell you how it's supposed to work. You're supposed to deescalate the situation. Do you know what that means?"

"Sure, I do. But it's easier said than done. Scott isn't

willing to back off."

"All right." Almeada took a seat in my client chair. "Let's go over the proper steps you need to take."

I already knew what I had to do, from making a formal complaint to documenting every occurrence. I had no intention of filing my own restraining order against the man. This was harassment, stalking, and property damage. Add in the death threats and abuse of power and, at the very least, Scott would be facing a suspension. At the most, jail time. Though, Almeada didn't believe we had enough evidence to pursue those charges yet.

"What's the bartender's name?" Almeada asked, making notes.

"Jim Harrelson, former police lieutenant."

"And he witnessed Renwin hit Jade?"

"He said it was dark. He doesn't want to get involved, but if push came to shove, he would testify."

Almeada nodded. "And the waitress? Melody, was it?"

"Yeah, but I bet most of the staff at KC's have stories to share." Maybe one of them gave me up to Renwin.

"All right. I'll have someone from the firm speak to them and see if this is worth pursuing. I already spoke to your assistant about the people who've launched complaints against Renwin. Honestly, if we push a little, we could take his job."

"We should."

"Probably, but my duty is to my client. Your duty is to your client. As soon as I put some things together, I'll reach out to Renwin's counsel and offer a quid pro quo. I'll stop digging into this and you'll back off if Renwin agrees to leave Jade alone. Deal?"

"And he goes to anger management."

Almeada chuckled. "Is that a sticking point for you?"

"If he wants to keep his badge, it is."

"Let me tell you something, Cross. It's not our problem if he does it again. We do our jobs. We do the best we can, and we pass it off. Problems like this are above our paygrades."

"No wonder you're a defense attorney."

"Yeah, well, it wasn't too long ago you were in need of

my services."

"Maybe I should have gone to anger management, then we wouldn't be here now."

Almeada laughed. "Regardless, everyone's entitled to equal protection under the law."

"Do you believe that?"

"Sure."

"I never knew you were an idealist. The system's fucked. It doesn't work the way it should."

"Once again, that's above my paygrade, but I do the best I can to even the odds."

I doubted it, but I kept my mouth shut.

TWENTY-TWO

The day was a blur. I rubbed my temples, hoping it would stop the throbbing in my head. Jade came into the living room with two mugs of green tea and a squeezable bear. She flipped the bear upside down and poured some honey into her tea before pushing it closer to me.

"Did Mr. Almeada pick up groceries?" I asked.

"The place came stocked. The bathrooms even have decorative soaps."

"I told you this place was nicer."

She blushed, stirring her tea anxiously. "About that. I...I will pay you back. Would it be okay if we set up a payment plan? I'm just not sure yet where I'm going to live. I can probably find a room or roommate, so rent should be more manageable. And once I get back to work, I can pick up some extra shifts and look for a second job."

"Stop. It's fine."

"Lucien, come on. This is your business. I don't want to be your charity case."

"Fine. Pay me back. Don't pay me back. I don't care. Just please," I stared at the spoon, "stop doing that."

Abruptly, she released the spoon and put the cup on the table. "I'm so sorry. I didn't mean..."

"Hey," I said softly, "look at me. It's okay. I just have a

headache. It's not a big deal. Honestly, if you wanted to run through the house banging the pots together, I wouldn't stop you. Though, I'd appreciate it if you refrain from doing that."

She studied me for the longest time, a newfound understanding dawning in her eyes. "I've forgotten what it's like to not live in fear."

I didn't have the heart to tell her what happened today with Scott. "We'll figure this out. But you're safe here. The building even has a doorman and its own security guards. Everything will be okay."

"Y'know, I think I'm starting to believe that." She let out a breath. "Mr. Almeada says we should be able to get my life back on track soon, and I can stay in the city if I choose."

"What do you want to do?"

"I don't know yet, but I need to save up some money before I make any decisions. Mr. Almeada said I should be able to get back to work in a couple of days, but you moved me here for a reason. At work, I'm a sitting duck. Scott's probably waiting there for me to show up."

"That's why your lawyer is offering Scott a truce if he agrees to leave you alone. We'll see what he says. Meanwhile, I just hired a dozen bodyguards who are undergoing training at the moment. Depending on how well they do in class, I might field test them. Would you mind being my guinea pig?"

"Actually, I'd feel better knowing someone was around." She looked at me with big doe eyes. "I thought you might guard me."

"I would, but since Scott's figured out you came to me for help, it's not in your best interest." I didn't go into the details of all the precautions I had to take just to get to the apartment. Like Almeada reminded me, my duty was to protect my client. So I was protecting her from the gruesome facts.

We fell silent, drinking our tea. I let my head fall back against the plush cushions and closed my eyes, feeling a constant buzz beneath my eyelids. Jade remained silent beside me, and I opened one eye to find her watching me.

"Do you have any clue how Scott found out you came to me for help?" I'd exhausted the most likely possibilities.

She shook her head. I waited, figuring if the question made her nervous or upset, she'd fidget or stir her tea, but her hands remained steady. "I did everything you said. Do you think he saw your car outside the apartment or maybe he checked with the people at the airport?"

"Could be."

"Is this a problem?"

"Not really." My four popped tires would disagree. "It just complicates matters."

"I'm sorry."

"It's not your fault. Stop apologizing." I rubbed my eyes. "Do you know if there's any aspirin in the bathroom?" Depending on the clients this apartment entertained, a few vials of coke or a bottle of oxy could be stashed somewhere inside. Neither of those would help matters in the long run. Short-term, they might do in a pinch, but I still had to stop by the precinct. And I didn't need to give Scott any reason to arrest me. I'd have to be squeaky clean until this was over. Plus, drugs were never my scene, minus an occasional recreational night here or there when work and play blurred into days without sleep.

"I'll check." She uncurled from her spot on the couch and disappeared down the hall before I had time to protest. A moment later she returned with a bottle of OTC pain relievers. "Migraine?"

"Just a headache."

"I used to get migraines a lot. Stress probably."

"Do you know if you ever had a concussion?"

She shook her head, uncomfortable with the question. "Probably not. I never hit my head."

"Concussions make migraines more likely, or so says an article I read."

She slipped behind the couch, and I tilted my head up and looked at her. "When I was little, my mom used to rub my temples whenever I was sick." Slowly, she reached for me, unsure if she should touch me. I didn't move or speak. I didn't want to frighten her. Her fingertips brushed against the sides of my face, and gently, she rubbed small circles with her pointer and middle fingers.

"Why didn't you go back home after things went south with Scott?"

"I was ashamed."

"I'm sorry."

"Why are you apologizing?" she asked, hoping to tease me, but her tone wasn't convincing. It wasn't her fault, but no matter how many times someone told her that, she felt guilty, embarrassed, and ashamed for not standing up for herself, for not stopping it, and for letting it go on as long as it did.

"No one should have to endure that. I'm sorry you did." Gently, I took her hand, and she stopped rubbing my temples.

For the first time since we met, she didn't pull away from my touch. She came around the couch and sat beside me. And then she hugged me.

TWENTY-THREE

After I left Jade's that night, the chauffeured car took me back to Reeves and Almeada where I collected my rental car, glad to find it with four fully inflated tires. I stopped by the precinct and filed a complaint against Sgt. Renwin for unprofessional and belligerent behavior. No one would take the complaint seriously since Renwin didn't actually do anything I could prove, but we needed to start a paper trail.

On my way home, a patrol car pulled me over. The officer wanted to search my vehicle, but I refused to comply. He had no grounds to conduct a search, and at this point, I feared what he might plant inside my car. He stared at my license and the rental agreement.

"Your name looks familiar." He hoped to sound menacing and make me squirm. Instead, I turned the tables on him.

"It should. My last name, anyway." I cleared my throat as the 'oh shit' look erupted on his face. "That's right. I'm *that* Lucien Cross."

"I'm sorry, sir. I didn't mean to inconvenience you. Make sure you report that messed up turn signal to the rental place when you return the car. And drive safe."

"Will do."

He handed back my documents. "You have a good night. I'm sorry for the misunderstanding."

"You and me both."

I planned to make another trip to KC's and drive by Scott's place to see what the bastard was up to, but after the day I had, I was too tired to do anything but sleep. The next morning, I found Scott parked outside my building. He didn't do or say anything, but he drove his truck so I would notice him. He wanted me to know he was watching and waiting. He was planning something. And that's when I realized he thought I stashed Jade at my place.

On the bright side, he wouldn't be motivated to look elsewhere. So I set my lights to go on and off at certain times while I was out to convince him his assumption was correct. The longer I maintained the ruse, the safer she'd be. Plus, he didn't have a chance in hell of gaining access to my apartment and learning the truth. Or so I told myself.

The rest of the week moved at a crawl. Cross Security remained empty. I fielded calls and signed a fourth client. I started on the background checks and combed Mr. Rathbone's servers for data breaches, completing the simpler tasks weeks ahead of schedule. Pleased, Rathbone assigned me another task, assessing his firewall and anti-hacking protocols. Though I'd already tested them when I checked his data security, I did it again.

Thursday, I dropped by the training facility and spoke to the instructor I hired. The security personnel passed all recommended requirements, fitness, firearms, first-aid, and crisis training. Since they already possessed the necessary skills, this was just a refresher and an introduction to my standards. I briefed them on their upcoming tasks.

The best and brightest would spend the next several weeks providing security for Miranda's tour. I spoke to her and said I'd send them over Saturday, so they could get acquainted. That left me with six people to guard Jade. Deciding to rotate them out to avoid Scott or another police officer recognizing them, I doled out assignments and called it training. I showed them a photo of Scott

Renwin and told them to keep their eyes peeled. I also made them painfully aware that they should not consider any police personnel who happened to wander into the diner as an ally, and if a situation arose, they should call 9-1-1 and let dispatch know they were reporting a crime on my behalf. Scott might have wanted to turn the entire police force against me, but my reach was far greater than his. It was one of the few perks of being a Cross.

On my way back to the office, Almeada called. "Renwin doesn't want any trouble."

"Do you believe him? The bastard's been lurking outside my apartment and office all week. I caught him going through my garbage yesterday."

"Did you confront him?"

"No."

"Do you think he'll be able to piece anything together?"

"From the confetti I discarded, definitely not."

"Have you encountered any other problems? Car or otherwise?"

"No."

"Good." Almeada paused. "The complaint you filed must have scared him. Your name carries weight. By now, he must have figured that out. I think that's why his attorney gave me his word Ms. McNamara would have no further contact with his client. They don't want trouble. And you, my friend, like to cause trouble."

"That's why it's not good for me to get twitchy. And Scott makes me twitchy."

"Take some diazepam and get over it. It looks like we've finally put this thing to bed. I reached out to the women's shelters in the area. They have funds and a network set up. They'll help Jade find a safe place to live, and they offer free counseling."

"Do you think she needs it?"

Almeada chuckled. "You tell me."

I did, but that wasn't my decision. It was hers. "Forcing it on anyone who isn't open to it is a waste of time, except in Scott's case. I don't give a shit what he wants. Since he still possesses a badge, he needs to learn the right way of conducting himself in public."

"That's the second time you've talked about therapy. I never thought Lucien Cross was this enlightened."

"Why not?"

Almeada practically choked. "It's because you're a little fucked in the head."

"That's called drive and ambition."

"That's called a chip on your shoulder."

I shrugged and parked the car. "I want it on record that I don't trust Scott Renwin."

"Noted. But you don't have to trust him, you just have to stop firing shots at him until we find out if he's serious about keeping his distance from Ms. McNamara."

"Only time will tell. Right now, she's focused on going back to work and overwhelmed by the possibility he might show up. Until we know for sure Scott's backing off, we need to focus on that. I'll have people watching her at the diner. If Scott or any of his buddies shows their ugly faces at the diner, there will be hell to pay."

For the first time in days, I didn't see the oversized pickup or a police car outside my office. I should have been relieved. Instead, not knowing where Scott was made me panicky. I didn't do well with twitchy, and panicky was far worse.

TWENTY-FOUR

Days went by. No one spotted Scott at the diner. Jade didn't see him or any of his friends. I kept tabs on him from a distance, not wanting to poke the sleeping beast. Since the hearing, he kept to himself.

I sent Justin into KC's to find out what was going on, but my assistant reported back Scott hadn't had a drink in almost a week. According to the agreement, he'd gone to every anger management session. Maybe they told him to stop drinking. Too much alcohol often led to heightened emotional responses and violence, so perhaps that would solve the problem. However, I wasn't optimistic.

I recalled my receptionist and assistant back to the office. Despite this hiccup, we still had a business to get off the ground. I scheduled a dozen meetings with potential clients and three interviews with tech-savvy applicants. At some point, I'd need more security specialists and analysts, but for now, overextending my resources could be disastrous. Even though I wanted to go from zero to sixty, new businesses thrived with baby steps, and since I didn't have any financial backers, I had total freedom to do what I wanted. But I had to pay for it myself. I wanted it all. Everything. Right now.

"Patience. Patience," I mumbled like a mantra.

"Mr. Cross, Sara Rostokowski is on line two," my receptionist called from the outer office.

"Thanks," I yelled back. "Next time, use the intercom."

"Sorry, sir."

I picked up the phone and pressed the button. "What's wrong, Sara?"

"Hey, I just thought you should know Sgt. Renwin resigned today. He cleaned out his desk and left."

"Any idea why?"

"According to the lieutenant, Renwin's tired of the city, so he's going home."

"But he's from here." I reached into the drawer and pulled out the dossier I made.

"Well, sort of. He grew up in the suburbs. His mom still lives in his childhood home. He wants to be close to her."

"It's twenty minutes away." It didn't make sense.

"Hey, I'm just telling you what I heard. The point is you wanted him off the force, and he's gone." She lowered her voice. "Did you have anything to do with that?"

"Not me, unless he came under pressure because of the TRO."

"I don't know. I heard there was a discussion about allowing him to continue to carry. But I don't know what they decided. Without a gun, he couldn't leave the station. He'd have to work dispatch or stay behind a desk. Maybe fulfill a civilian role. I think that's why he quit."

"He did it to himself."

"If he's as bad as you say, then good riddance. The last thing any of us needs is another misogynistic asshole beating up women."

"Thanks for the heads up." The news left a bad taste in my mouth. I called the security specialist stationed at the diner and told him to remain vigilant. Then I asked Justin if I could borrow his car and headed to Scott's apartment.

Parking a few blocks away, I remained crouched in the seat, watching the former police sergeant load boxes and furniture into the back of the pickup. He dragged Jade's futon to the dumpster. Then he loaded a few more boxes into the cab and got behind the wheel.

Once he drove away, I went to his apartment and knocked on the door. No one answered, so I tried the knob. The door opened without protest. The apartment was empty. No furniture. No boxes. Nothing. He took everything. He wasn't coming back.

After speaking to the landlord, I was assured this wasn't a ploy. Scott quit his job and gave up his apartment. On the way back to the office, I made several calls to area storage rentals. Scott didn't rent a unit. He actually left the city.

But I didn't believe it. I called Almeada, who promised to look into the matter. Since Scott had a change of address, he was required to notify the court since he had mandated anger management sessions. If nothing else, Scott's lawyer would have his forwarding address.

However, I wasn't one to wait. Call it impatience or attributes of a workaholic, but I'd find the answers faster on my own. Plus, I'd have to see it to believe it. I returned Justin's car to the office and scoured the internet until my vision blurred.

Around ten that night, I drove to the suburbs. Mrs. Renwin lived in a quiet neighborhood. Scott's truck took up the length of the small driveway. The furniture and boxes had been unloaded. Despite the time, the blinds remained open, and I could see Scott and a woman sitting at the kitchen table.

Two thoughts formed simultaneously. First, Jade was finally free. And second, that bastard better not lay a hand on his mother. Unwilling to accept the win, I found a house for rent at the end of the street and parked in the driveway. I kept my eyes on the Renwins' place until Mrs. Renwin left the next morning.

Starting my engine, I followed her to the supermarket. I didn't have a plan. In fact, I had no idea what I was doing. I parked near her car and peered into the windows as I passed. I didn't know what I hoped to find, but it wasn't here.

Following her through the store, I pushed a cart and spent a lot of time reading the ingredients on a box of cereal. She didn't notice me. I went down the next aisle, grabbing some paper towels and a box of matches.

"Excuse me," I said, bumping into her cart.

She looked up, smiling warmly. A gesture her son appeared incapable of performing. "It's quite all right." I turned up the charm and asked her if she could tell me where I could pick up some flowers. "They have a floral section near the bakery." She pointed to the other end of the store. "Are you shopping for anyone special? Your wife or girlfriend?"

"Actually, I was on my way to visit my mom. She doesn't get out much, so I bring her groceries every week and thought I'd get something to brighten her day."

"You're a good son."

"I try." Quickly, I assessed her, hoping to find an opening to ask about her own son. "Do you have any idea what she might like? I can't decide between a plant or flowers. The plant will last longer, but flowers are prettier."

"Whatever you get, she will love." She stepped closer, and I crouched down to hear her better. "I'm not much of a plant person. My Scottie usually just brings something sweet for us to eat."

"It sounds like he has the right idea."

"The cakes here are delicious, especially the rocky road one, if you like chocolate. In fact, Scottie brought one over last night."

"I'll have to check those out." I turned back to the shelf, grabbing a box of tissues and glancing up to read the signs. "It sounds like the two of you are close."

"I have a lot to make up for. I'm lucky we have this time to catch up."

TWENTY-FIVE

The following night, I went to KC's and spoke to Will, Melody, and some of the regulars. As far as they knew, Scott was gone. He wanted to start over and reinvent himself. Their stories differed, as one would expect from rampant rumors and gossip, but everyone agreed he left and didn't plan on returning.

When I spoke to Almeada the next morning, he said, "According to Scott's attorney, all future correspondence will be sent to his mother's address. It looks like we won."

"What did we win?"

"Don't be so literal. Jade gets peace of mind, and you can get back to your plans for world domination."

"Scott's not that far away. Without traffic, he can get back to the city in twenty minutes. This doesn't mean a damn thing."

"You don't get it, Cross. Sure, he's close, but he won't be getting his coffee or bagel from his usual spot. He won't be riding the trains or buses. It's unlikely he'll cross paths with Jade now that he doesn't live in the city."

"If you say so." I could practically hear Almeada roll his eyes. "But I'm leaving a protection team at the diner, just in case."

"That's your dime. Just make sure she doesn't think you're stalking her."

"I'm not."

Almeada laughed. "I'm joking. Lighten up."

I growled at him and hung up.

After my meetings for the day, I called Jade. She had been in contact with one of the shelters. They found her an apartment and a roommate, another woman who'd escaped an abusive relationship. The roommate worked at the shelter and mentored other abused women. It sounded like the ideal situation.

"I told her I'd check out the place after my shift, and if I like it, I can move in this weekend."

"That's fantastic." I picked up a pen. "What's this lady's name?"

"Why?"

"Am I overstepping if I say I want to run a background check?"

"Yes, but I'd appreciate it." She gave me the woman's name and address. "I'll call you when I leave her place. I thought maybe we could get dinner. I want to properly thank you for everything you've done to help me."

"That's not necessary."

"Please," she whined, "it's the least I can do."

"Okay."

That was the first night Jade went out since escaping Scott. We sat in the corner booth, near an emergency exit, and shared fajitas and drank way too much tequila. Unlike me, Jade wanted to celebrate her freedom. She missed living, or so she kept saying. She missed being carefree and fun. She missed herself. She had lost who she was along the way, and now she was tired of the person she had become. She hated being afraid, but it didn't keep her eyes from darting to the door every time someone entered the restaurant.

"He's gone," I said finally.

"I know. Mr. Almeada gave me the news this afternoon. It's why he said it was safe to go out on my own."

"How's work?"

"Fine. Scott never stopped by. The only time a police

officer came inside was to order a sandwich to go. I didn't recognize him."

"Well, the police department employs thousands of men and women. You won't recognize most of them."

"You're right." She brushed her fiery red hair behind her ear. "I'm ready to put this behind me. I don't want to talk about it or think about it anymore." She held up a set of keys. "I told Mary Beth I wanted to share the apartment, if she'd have me. She said yes."

"That's great."

Those teal eyes burned into my soul. "You should tell that to your face."

I forced a smile to my lips. "I do think it's great. See?" I picked up the shot glass and tipped it back. "Everything checked out. Mary Beth's clean. The neighborhood's safe. Just don't get stuck. You said you didn't know what you wanted to do yet, so keep your options open."

"I will."

"Okay." When the check came, I reached for my wallet, but Jade swatted my hand.

"This is my treat, remember?" She counted out some crumpled bills, probably her tip money from today, and paid for dinner.

"You don't have to do that."

"Yes, I do. And I am planning to pay you back. Just let me get some things together first."

"No rush." I called for a car to pick us up. Despite the fact the danger was removed, I felt uneasy. It would pass eventually, just not tonight.

"Explain something to me. What kind of P.I. takes a case without getting paid, incurs a ton of expenses, and wages war with the police department?"

"The kind who doesn't know what he's doing. Like I told you when we met, I just opened my security firm. This was my first and only investigation. Hell, I wasn't even licensed when I agreed to help you. Just don't report me."

She stared open-mouthed at me. "I'm glad you didn't tell me this in the coffee shop. I wouldn't have trusted you."

"You didn't trust me." I watched her closely. "You still don't."

"I don't trust anyone, Lucien. Not completely. But I'm working on it. I'd like to trust you."

The way she licked her lips and brushed her hair away from her face made me yearn for that trust and whatever benefits might go along with it, but that wouldn't be professional. I could lose my license. Maybe. Actually, I didn't know, especially since she wasn't a paying client. However, that would probably make it worse. Either way, it didn't matter. That was the tequila talking.

When we arrived at the apartment, I walked her to her door. She unlocked it, and I stepped inside to make sure it was safe. Once I knew the coast was clear, I bid her goodnight and had the driver take me home. *Leaving is the right thing to do,* I kept telling myself. But had I not been so distracted, I might have noticed the car parked at the end of the street.

TWENTY-SIX

I'd gotten home three hours ago, convinced I'd fall asleep the second my head hit the pillow. Instead, I stared at the ceiling. The tequila must have triggered my insomnia. I thought about getting up to work, but I didn't feel like it. My thoughts lingered on Jade. When the phone rang, I reached for it, figuring an ex-girlfriend wanted to hook up for the night.

The number on the display sent chills through me. "What's wrong?" I asked, already out of bed and rapidly dressing.

"I heard a noise at the window. I thought I saw him."

"Scott?" I zipped my fly and secured my holster. "Did you call building security?"

"Yes."

"What did they say?" I grabbed my keys and ran to the elevator.

Jade inhaled a shaky breath. "They didn't see anyone. A couple of guys went outside to look around, and someone else is checking the security feed."

"Did anyone call the police?"

"I don't know. I didn't want to, but they might have."

"All right. I'm on my way. Where are you? Are you in the apartment?"

"No, I'm sitting in the security office."

"Okay." The guards inside the building were armed. They'd keep Jade safe.

"Lucien, don't hang up."

"I'm not. I'm right here." I put the phone on speaker, relieved I'd gotten my tires fixed since I returned the rental car several days ago. The apartment where Jade was staying was on the third floor. It didn't have a fire escape or balcony. "Where do you think you saw Scott?"

"Standing on the corner, across the street."

"Did you see his truck?"

"No."

What did his mother drive? I wracked my brain, but in my frazzled state I couldn't think what kind of car it was. "What about a silver four-door?"

Jade repeated the question, presumably to the security guard. "There are six parked on the street. Can you be more specific?"

"Hang on." I tried to enter the vehicle search into my phone, but I couldn't do it while on a call. Not to mention, I shouldn't be doing that while driving. "I don't know. Do you know what his mom's car looks like?"

"Y'know, I never met his mother." Jade's tone sounded odd. "That should have tipped me off. What kind of man doesn't want you to meet his mother?"

I wouldn't want to bring anyone home to my mother, but I didn't share that thought. Approaching the apartment, I drove up and down the street, checking each vehicle, but I didn't recognize any of them. "I'm on my way in. I'll see you in a sec."

Disconnecting, I phoned the precinct, reported a disturbance, and entered the lobby. The night manager recognized me, gesturing to the security office in the back corner. Nodding, I knocked on the door before opening it.

"Hey," Jade said, relief flooding over her.

"It's okay," I said quietly before turning my attention to the guard. "All right. What do we know?"

"Mr. Cross," he slid his chair over, and I leaned over his shoulder, checking the monitor, "as you can see, the building hasn't been breached. We didn't spot any suspicious activity outside." His radio squawked, and he picked it up, listening to the all-clear message come from the two guards he sent outside to patrol. He looked sympathetically at Jade. "Is it possible you were dreaming?"

"I don't know," she admitted. "I was in bed when I heard tapping at the window."

"Tapping? Like a bird?" I asked.

"Not really. It was quieter and not nearly as consistent."

The guard gave me a look, and I glowered at him. "Let's speak outside for a moment." I practically pushed him into the lobby. "You're probably right to assume she imagined it, but we're taking precautions anyway. Mr. Almeada told you to expect as much, so don't act surprised or put out. I called the police and reported a disturbance. When they show up, I'll speak to them, but I suspect they'll have questions for you and your guys. Answer them truthfully." I held out a photograph of Scott Renwin. "This is who we're looking for. He might even show up in a police uniform. So we're going to be careful and smart about this. Understand?"

"Whatever you say, sir."

I narrowed my eyes. Building security thought I was a joke. But I didn't have the time or energy to rip him a new one. "Fine. Just let me know when the police get here, and please cooperate with them. Until then, Ms. McNamara and I will wait in her apartment. Let's just hope I don't have to report this to her lawyer in the morning."

That got his attention. "Yes, sir."

I led Jade upstairs, wary of our surroundings. She opened her mouth to apologize, but caught herself, and laughed. Once inside, I checked the hidden cameras I set up near the doorway. Since there was only one way in and out, I knew no one had gained entry.

"Which window?"

"The one in the kitchen." She pointed. "I was in bed, but I couldn't sleep."

"I know the feeling."

"What keeps you up?" The question sounded innocent, but her lips quirked mischievously in the corner.

I rubbed my eyes. Maybe I was still drunk or dreaming. Either way, the question didn't require a response. Checking the kitchen window, I turned off the lights and peered out the slats in the blinds. But I didn't see anything.

"What did it sound like?"

"A pebble hitting the window."

"How many times did it happen?"

"Three or four. I wouldn't have gotten up to check if it was just once."

But I didn't see any pebbles on the ledge or cracks in the glass. I rummaged around the rest of the kitchen, wondering if something else might have made the sound. I even checked for leaky faucets. The intercom buzzed, and I went to the door.

"Yes?"

"Mr. Cross, you wanted me to let you know when the police arrived."

"I'm on my way."

"The police?" Jade swallowed, ready to bolt.

"Shh," I soothed, "I want them to take a look around. Paper trails, remember?"

She nodded but didn't look convinced.

"Stay here. Lock the doors. I'll be back soon."

After I spoke to a few patrolmen and explained the situation, they promised to keep an eye out, but no one had seen Scott or anyone else lurking around outside. The only people who'd entered the apartment building lived here, and the cars parked outside all had permits. If I had other investigators working for me, I'd have sent one of them to keep an eye on Mrs. Renwin's house and make sure Scott was there, but I didn't. Instead, I called my assistant at three a.m. and asked him to drive over and see if anything appeared out of place.

Justin threatened to quit, something he did on occasion to remind me I was an insufferable prick, but agreed to go. I went back upstairs and let myself into Jade's apartment. "It's normal to be anxious. A lot has changed. But no one's seen anything suspicious."

She nodded. "I know. I didn't mean to drag you out in the middle of the night, or involve the authorities, or drive building security crazy."

"Considering how much Reeves and Almeada spend on this place, building security can get over it." I gave her a reassuring smile. "You're safe. He isn't out there, but just to be sure, I sent Justin to drive by his mom's house and make sure everything looks normal."

"Okay."

Thirty minutes later, he called and told me everything was quiet. Scott's truck remained in the driveway, and he spotted a car parked inside the garage. I didn't want to know what he did to find that out, but I thanked him, told him to take the day off, and promised a nice bonus in this week's check.

"I should go. You need to get some sleep." I looked out the window a final time. "No one's coming for you tonight."

Before I could turn around, she ran her palms down my arms. "Don't leave me alone, Lucien."

"Jade, you'll be okay. You don't need me to stick around."

"What if I want you to?"

"I guess that's a different story."

I didn't instigate. I didn't touch her. I let her take the lead. She wanted to regain control of her life. She deserved to be pleasured, worshipped, and made to feel special and safe, so for the rest of the night, I let her use my body however she desired. And I enjoyed every minute of it.

TWENTY-SEVEN

The sheet skimmed her alabaster skin. Her face relaxed. The worry and tension erased as she slept, making her appear younger, more like the woman from the photo. For the first time, I noticed a few faint freckles dotting her nose, brought out by the red of her hair. I didn't touch her. Even after the night we had, I knew she wouldn't appreciate the contact. I hoped one day she'd be able to accept affection without fear.

Silently, I got out of bed and dressed. It was seven. I should be on my way to the office, but for the first time in my life, sneaking out of someone's apartment didn't feel right. Luckily, I told Justin to take the day off, so he couldn't give me grief about this. After sending a text to my receptionist to reschedule my morning meetings, I made coffee and checked the fridge.

The bare shelves stared back at me, so I ordered breakfast from the café down the street, left Jade a note that I'd be right back, and went to pick up our food. The neighborhood looked different in the daylight. Less menacing, more family-friendly. Several women pushed strollers down the sidewalk. A few men walked dogs, and a couple of joggers ran past. I tried to get out of the way, bumping into one jogger with a hoodie.

"Sorry," I muttered, but he just kept going.

After picking up breakfast, I stopped by the security office to make sure nothing else happened during the course of the night, but the men I'd spoken to had gone home, replaced by the next shift. Since no police cruisers were parked outside, I assumed they didn't find anything either. However, our city's finest had better things to do than worry about prowlers or the cause of unknown disturbances.

Reaching into my pocket, I didn't find my set of keys to the apartment. I must have left them on the counter next to my phone and coffee. Obviously, Jade screwed my brains out. I chuckled, not wanting to knock on the door and wake her. But she might wonder where I was. After debating for far too long, I finally knocked.

"Jade," I said, "it's me."

She came to the door in a towel, her hair wet from the shower. "You didn't have to get breakfast."

"It seemed only fair." Fighting the urge to kiss her, I did my best to appear charming as I set the containers on the counter. She went into the bedroom to dress, and I stared out the window. She was right, all the silver cars looked alike from here.

When the hairdryer stopped, I pulled plates from the cupboard and put them on the table. Then I made her a fresh cup of coffee. While it brewed, I cleaned up the mess I left, putting my phone in my pocket and hooking my holster to the side of my belt. Frowning, I checked my pockets again.

"What's wrong?" she asked, stepping into the kitchen.

"I can't find my keys."

"Did you leave them in the bedroom? I thought I saw your watch on the nightstand."

"I'll check." Just as I moved past her, she grabbed the front of my shirt and pulled me into her for a kiss. "Good morning."

"Good morning," she whispered.

I went into the bedroom, finding my watch where she said it was. While I fastened it around my wrist, I looked in the nightstand drawer and beneath the bed, but I didn't spot my keys. Maybe I left them in the security office last night, but I was almost certain I unlocked the door.

"Did you find them?"

"No." Missing keys posed a problem. Despite the doorman and building security, the attached fob could get anyone inside the building. This wasn't good. "I know I had them last night." I checked the recorded footage from the cameras I set up inside the apartment. I was the only person who entered or left. "I'll check downstairs and see if security has them."

"It can't wait until after breakfast?" Jade asked.

"It'll only take a minute." I went out the door and retraced my steps, wondering if I dropped them along the way.

When the elevator opened in the lobby, I stepped out. Two women in yoga gear stood near the doors chatting, and a jogger stretched just outside the doors. I spoke to the manager, but he didn't see my keys.

"Let me know if someone finds them."

Next, I knocked on the door to the security office. The guard looked up, snickering. I only left him a few minutes ago.

"Back so soon?" he asked. He eyed my empty hands. "I hoped you decided to bring me breakfast."

"Next time," I mumbled. I searched the top of his desk and the chair cushions. "Have you seen a set of keys?"

"Yeah. I put them somewhere around here."

Resisting the urge to roll my eyes, I blew out a slow breath while I watched the man rummage around in the filing cabinet. "Welcome to the lost and found." The sarcastic comment did nothing to improve my mood. Five minutes later, he produced a fancy set of car keys with a soccer ball keychain.

"Those aren't mine." Practically shoving him out of the way, I peered into the drawer as a growing unease built inside of me. "Dammit." I slammed the drawer shut. "Tell the doorman not to let anyone into the building he doesn't recognize." I patted my pockets again, suddenly remembering the jogger who'd bumped into me. Or did I bump into him? "Shit."

Leaving the office, I ran to the stairwell, taking the steps two at a time. I burst onto the third floor, finding the apartment door open. "Jade?" The apartment looked like it did before I left. "Jade?" I tried again, a desperation clawing at my insides. She wouldn't have left the door open.

I checked each of the rooms. She wasn't here, and my car keys were gone. I went around the kitchen counter to grab the tablet and access the surveillance footage, and that's when I spotted the shattered coffee cup. With shaking hands I played back the footage, knowing exactly what I'd see.

TWENTY-EIGHT

"He's got her. That bastard took her. Get everyone on this now," I barked into my phone as I ran full speed down the steps. I burst into the lobby, spotting a streak of red just beyond the front door. "Stop them." The doorman turned to see what the commotion was. "That man in the hoodie. Stop him." I sprinted across the lobby, shoving the chatting women out of my way.

The doorman was a few steps ahead of me. The two security guards were a few feet behind. But Scott had too much of a head start. He shoved Jade into my car, forcing her across the front seats before getting in. I ran toward them, but he peeled away from the curb, clipping me with the front fender as he barreled down the street.

"Sir, are you all right?" the doorman asked. He stopped pursuit the moment Scott and Jade got into the car. "I called 9-1-1."

"Tell them to issue a BOLO on Scott Renwin. He's driving a black Mercedes. He's with Jade McNamara." I rattled off my license plate number.

The police would never find them in time. Scott would ditch the car the first chance he got. I had to get to him first. I called Justin the moment I realized she was gone.

He would have already called the police. They should be on their way. He'd tell them everything they needed to know, so I didn't need to waste my time here.

Grabbing my phone, I entered my PIN and accessed my car's GPS. Scott had a plan. I'd known it all along. Unfortunately, I didn't know what it was. I couldn't just stand here and watch him get farther away. Jogging up the street, I spotted Mrs. Renwin's silver four-door parked on a side street, concealed behind an SUV. I grabbed my gun, wondering why I didn't shoot the bastard before he drove away, but I didn't think. Why didn't I think?

Turning my head, I thrust my gun against the window and reached in to unlock the door. The private investigator who mentored me taught me how to hotwire a car, and after a few attempts, the engine roared to life. Pulling out of the space, I kept one eye on the road and the other on my phone. I had to get to Jade.

They were still driving, so I had to assume as long as they were on the road, she was safe. Well, as safe as she could be with an unstable and violent man behind the wheel. Stomping down on the gas, I zipped in and out of traffic. The other vehicles on the road became nothing more than a blur. I ran the red, narrowly avoiding a pedestrian in the crosswalk and a delivery truck heading straight toward me.

"Where are you going, Scott?" I looked at the tiny map, hoping to decipher the few street names and route numbers. It didn't look familiar. At first, I thought he might be taking Jade back to his mother's house, but he was headed in the wrong direction. Maybe their apartment? But he was too far east for that.

I looked up just in time to slam on the brakes. Angry horns blared, and I swallowed and cursed. Damn light. I waited, feeling Jade slipping away as the seconds passed. I promised I'd keep her safe. I should have never said that. I shouldn't have taken the case. Maybe I should have gone to my father for help.

As soon as the light changed, I lurched forward. The sedan bumped and grinded in protest, but I didn't ease up on the gas. By now, Scott had abandoned my car, possibly to switch cars. If he did, I'd never find them. But even getting stuck at the red light didn't put me too far behind. I found my Mercedes parked at a gas station with the doors open.

After quickly checking inside, not finding blood or any indication of where Scott might have taken her, I stepped inside. "Have you seen a red-haired woman and a man? They got out of that car." I pointed out the window.

The clerk looked up. "No."

I spun. "What about you?" I asked the guy in a trucker hat.

"Yeah, strangest thing. I saw them cross the street and go into that motel." He pointed. "I tried to tell him he left his door open, but it looked like they were in a rush, if you know what I mean."

"Call the cops. Tell them to get here now. We have a hostage situation." I didn't know if Scott was armed, but I knew those words would get the police department here quickly.

But no matter how fast they got here, I couldn't wait. Jade's life was in jeopardy. After entering the motel office, I went straight to the check-in desk. "What room is this man in?" I showed the clerk a photo of Scott. He just shook his head, so I pulled out my wallet and dumped out my cash. "What room?"

"Seventeen."

"I need a key."

"I can't do that."

I drew my weapon and aimed at him. "Fine." The clerk handed me a key. If Trucker Hat didn't call the cops, the motel clerk would.

Marching down the path, I tried to peer into the window, but I couldn't see inside. Scott must know staying in one spot would make him a sitting duck. He knew I'd seen him. Why wasn't he running?

I unlocked the door slowly. Cracking it open, I listened. Suddenly, a crash sounded from the back of the room.

"Jade?" My muscles tensed.

"Him?" Scott bellowed from the table beside the bed. He had an automatic machine pistol in his hand. "You left me for him? I love you. How could you do this to us? Why? Why would you fuck him?"

"Scott, please," she whimpered. She edged backward, knocking the in-room coffeemaker off the counter in her haste. The sound made her jump. But it didn't slow him down.

"I gave up everything for you. And you do this?"

"Stay away from her." I moved deeper into the room, intercepting him before he could get close to her. He took a step back, swinging the gun in my direction. "You shouldn't be here, Scott. The police are on the way. You need to leave. Now."

"You shouldn't be here," he growled. "You did this. You poisoned her mind. You made her file the court order." He shoved the hood of the sweatshirt off his head and stared at me with rage-filled eyes. He'd been outside Jade's apartment all night. She didn't imagine it. She saw him. "I've been watching you, Cross. I knew it. I knew you were fucking my girlfriend. You couldn't find your own woman, so you had to steal mine. Did you really think I was going to sit back and let that happen?"

"Back off."

"Drop your gun, or I'll shoot her and then you."

"She means nothing to me. I don't care. You point that at her, and I'll blow you away. So don't be stupid. Point it at me. Aim at me."

He thought for a moment, realizing I posed more of a threat, so he aimed at me while edging closer to her.

"You don't want to throw your life away. Think about this, man. You got your mom. You have the opportunity to start over, to fix things. You know what happens to cops who end up in prison. Just walk away. We'll pretend this didn't happen," I said.

"I'm not going to prison." He stared at me. "I did my homework on you." He laughed, an ugly, bitter sound. "No wonder you wanted to bed that bitch." He moved toward Jade, and I sidestepped, blocking his view. If he wanted her, he'd have to go through me. "You didn't have the balls to make it through the academy, not even with daddy's help. But it was daddy's help that kept you from going to prison when you nearly beat that guy to death." He looked over my shoulder at Jade. "Bet he didn't tell you that, babe." The anger contorted his already unattractive face into something hideous. "Guess you have a type, huh?"

"Hey, your problem is with me. That's right. I took your girl. I took your job. I took everything from you. So come on, let's settle this like men. Or are you afraid you can't take me in a fair fight?" If only I could distract him, she could get to safety.

"Lucien," Jade whimpered, edging along the counter.

I needed to keep him contained between the bed and the wall long enough for her to make it safely out of the room. Right now, she was as far from the front door as possible, and with the machine pistol in his hand, her chances of getting out of the room unscathed or even alive were minimal. So I'd have to improvise.

"Shut up, woman. Did I tell you to speak?" I hated saying it, but I needed him to believe she didn't act on her own. That it was my fault she left him. It was her only chance of surviving.

"I would have ended this in your office, but you wouldn't tell me where you hid her. Now you're going to regret it." Scott sneered.

"Wait, Scott, please. Forgive me. I'll go with you. We can go back to the way we were before. The way things were before I met him. Please," she said. "I'm sorry. I'm so sorry."

"You should be sorry." His finger remained tensed over the trigger. He had no intention of backing down, and I realized I missed something. Scott Renwin didn't move back in with his mother. He gave her his things and said his goodbyes. This wasn't an abduction. It was a murder-suicide.

"Jade, get down," I ordered.

Before the words even left my lips, he opened fire. I dove on top of her, aware of the deafening gunfire, her trembling body, and the screams. Everything dimmed, and when the darkness faded, the gunfire stopped. His boot squeaked on the tile floor. Instinct took over, along with some residual police academy training, and I fired in his direction. I tried to aim, but I couldn't lift my arm high enough. The first bullet went into his thigh, and the second went right into his ugly face.

"Jade?" I tried to lift myself off of her, but my arm slipped in the blood. Blood? I blinked, seeing several gaping holes in her leg. "Jade, hang on."

I reached down and pressed against one spot, and that's when I saw the river of red running down my arm. I stared at it, uncomprehending, and then like a bolt of lightning I was hit with a wave of excruciating pain. It took my breath, dimmed the lights, and made thought impossible. My muscles gave out. My nerves fried. My body in shock but no longer to the point of numbing me. I collapsed on top of her. The last thing I saw was what remained of that asshole's face.

TWENTY-NINE

"Clear."

At least I thought I heard someone say it. It sounded like an echo. A faint murmur, followed by a massive convulsion and my body levitating off the table as the fire burned through me. I gasped.

"He's back. Let's get him into surgery before he codes again. How many are we looking at?"

"Eight, no wait. Two grazes, and one through and through, so five."

"Careful when you roll him. We don't know if his spinal cord's compromised."

I moaned.

"He's coming out of it. Push another—"

I didn't hear what they said. "Jade?" I asked, frantic. "Jade?" I didn't even have the strength to open my eyes. Did I even speak aloud? Everything dimmed into nothingness.

The next time I regained consciousness, bright white lights blinded me. It took my eyes a few minutes to adjust, and I stared at the speckled tile. A blue plastic thing took up half my vision, but I couldn't figure out what it was.

I couldn't move. I just lay there, staring at the floor,

wondering where I was and what was happening. And then I drifted off again.

A sharp tickle at the bottom of my foot woke me. I jerked my leg, feeling something pull in my back. I was too numb to feel the pain, but somehow, I knew it hurt. The blue tube didn't impede my vision this time, and I saw a metal bar and white sheet. I tried to turn, but I couldn't move off my stomach. Honestly, I could barely breathe, let alone keep my eyes open.

"Mr. Cross," a kind voice said, "you're in the hospital. Do you remember what happened?" A man in a lab coat sat on a stool and rolled closer until I could see his face. "I'm Dr. Bashala."

"Jade? Where's Jade?"

"She's okay. The surgery went well. She's lucky. None of the bullets impacted with her bones. She should be back on her feet soon. The two of you were lucky."

"Lucky? Are you out of your freaking mind?"

The doctor stifled a laugh. "If her boyfriend hadn't found you, you might be dead."

"He tried to kill us." I tried to push myself up. This time, the pain broke through the numbness, and I crumpled against the thin mattress.

"Easy, you weren't nearly as fortunate. You need to rest. We'll talk more later."

"The police," I fought to keep my eyes open, "I need to speak to the police. And Almeada."

"They're in the waiting area. Everyone's pulling for you, son. You need to sleep now. Once we move you out of ICU, you can talk to whoever you want."

*   *   *

"This is bullshit." I glared at the police commissioner. "That's not what happened, and I can prove it. Sgt. Shithead stalked Jade, illegally entered the apartment, abducted her, and shot us both. We weren't attacked by a heavily armed unsub. Scott didn't come to our rescue. He came to kill us. Do you want to know who killed him? I did, and that's why."

Almeada gave me a sharp look, but I ignored it.

"It was self-defense. I have security footage to prove it. This," I gestured, disgusted, at the statement the commissioner wanted me to sign, "is a cover-up. I'm not signing that."

"Lucien, you need to think very carefully about your next move," the commissioner warned. "This is a lot of money. It's the best you're gonna get."

"It's blood money. You make me sick. Jade didn't sign, and neither am I."

"Your girlfriend should reconsider. With her expenses and medical bills, she could use the money. Or are you planning to support her the rest of your life?" the commissioner asked.

My expression soured further. "You have no right to insert yourself into my life or make my decisions for me. I'm a man, Dad. I can take care of myself. And my relationship with Jade is none of your business. She's not my girlfriend. She's a client."

"Cross," Almeada warned, "Renwin put some contingencies in place. He left some things behind that could confuse a jury." He flipped through the terms of the settlement. "Don't forget, you threatened the motel clerk with a gun. This is a good deal. Even if we won in court, you'd probably only be awarded a fraction of this. Juries are fickle. I suggest you at least consider taking the settlement. Just imagine what you could do with this kind of money."

Ignoring my attorney, I said, "Do you think you can buy my silence? That you can just pay me to go away again, like you've done my entire life?" I stared at my father, the police commissioner. "It's your job to make sure the men and women under your command protect this city. Police corruption, brutality, violence, murders, they happen. They happen a lot. And you aren't doing a damn thing about it. But somehow, you thought I'd be bad for the department. I guess you were right, and I'm about to prove it. Even though you made sure I washed out of the academy, you don't have the power to wash this away. I won't let you make that monster out to be a hero just so you can save face."

"Lucien, don't you get it? I wanted better for you than the life of a cop. It's not that you couldn't do the job, but you could do much more if you actually took a moment to explore your options. Now look at you. You're a business genius and driven. You can do whatever you want. This money will let you do whatever you want. You could expand that little security firm of yours or run a startup. Whatever. The sky's the limit. I spoke to the mayor and city council. This is the best deal you're gonna get. We maxed out the budget to make this happen. Just think about it. I'm not buying your silence. I'm trying to repent for my mistakes."

"Keep trying," I snapped.

My father walked out the door, leaving me fuming. I turned my head and stared out the window.

Almeada gave me a few minutes to cool off before he said, "He's right, you know."

"Yeah. I know. But that doesn't mean I have to like it."

THIRTY

"Is everything set?" I asked. "You put Jade's name on the account, right?"

"Yes, Mr. Cross."

"Great. Thanks." I hung up and carefully stretched.

Rehab and physical therapy left me sore every day. But I was getting stronger and more flexible. Justin would hate having to relinquish my office back to me next week. I owed him everything. If it weren't for him, Cross Security would have come to a crashing halt, but he kept business booming during these last few months. Drawing up a new contract and giving him a stake in my company felt fitting. I believed in rewarding hard work and loyalty. And Justin earned every penny.

My front door opened, and I turned my head, wincing at the sudden movement. A flash of red moved toward me, and I smiled. "Hey, babe."

Jade kissed me. "Sorry, I'm late. I picked up an extra shift. How did today go? What did the doctor say?"

"I'm fine. I can go back to work next week."

She nodded, her eyes a little sad. "I guess it's time."

"Hey, it's okay. This is what you want. If you change your mind, you can always come back."

"Are you sure I can't persuade you to come with me?" She looked hopeful. "I just don't think staying in the city is a good idea. I spoke to my folks. I need to get away from here, away from him, and everything that reminds me of him."

"Even me."

"No. Not you."

We talked about it a lot. Jade had been speaking to the counselors at the women's shelter and her roommate. She wanted to piece her life back together, but first, she had to figure out who she was. She couldn't do that here. And she didn't need me or anyone else getting in the way.

"I set up an account with your half of the settlement."

"Lucien, it's not my money. I didn't agree to the terms. You did. I don't want hush money. I don't want anything from that man. I'm done. I washed my hands of it. But if I decide to one day tell my story, I don't want some court order telling me I can't. This happened to me. And if speaking out will help someone else, then maybe I'll do it."

"Are you mad I took the money?"

She shook her head. "I just don't want any part of it."

"But I heard you talking to Mary Beth. You want to start your own not-for-profit to help victims of domestic violence. You need capital. Why not let some good come from this?"

"Why won't you take no for an answer?"

"Because I'm stubborn like that."

"It's too much. I wouldn't even know what to do with millions of dollars. I want you to take it and invest it in Cross Security. You can do more good than I can. You want to privatize policing. Just imagine how many people you can help."

"I want to do more than that." A dark cloud settled over me. I already pulled strings to get invited to a symposium where several well-respected federal law enforcement and private security officials would be speaking. Since I planned to do this, I wanted to do it right. "But I know how to build my business. I'll get there eventually. I don't need your money to do it."

"I want you to invest it in Cross Security. You saved my life, Lucien, and my quality of life. I owe you everything."

"No, you don't." I handed her the account information

for a checking account I opened for her. "This is just a fraction of the proceeds. I spoke to a few investment bankers I know. Interest and dividends will be deposited every month. It should be enough to support you until you get settled in Colorado. But as soon as you say the word, I will wire you the rest with interest. I don't care that you didn't take the settlement. This is your money. You're just letting me borrow it." I smirked. "Just promise me you won't buy a pot shop."

She laughed. "I'll try not to."

After dinner, I went with her to the tattoo parlor where Kai put the finishing touches on the leopard tattoo she got to hide the still healing scars. The doctors told her to wait, but she couldn't. Seeing the scars every day broke her heart and tore at her soul. She needed to rid herself of Scott Renwin and the terrible memories he left her. It's why she had to leave, and why I wouldn't stop her.

The next morning, I took her to the airport. We didn't speak much, but she held my hand. Something she normally didn't do.

"It's like the first day we met."

"You've come a long way," I said. "You're safe now."

She studied me. "Lucien, just be careful. Ever since that day, there's a darkness about you. It scares me. You're angry. You want revenge. The same thing happened to Scott before he turned into a monster. It isn't worth it." She took my face in her hands. "Don't turn into a monster."

"I won't."

She smiled. "I guess you're nothing more than a fallen angel."

"Wouldn't that make me the devil?"

"Then find your grace. Forgive and move on." She smiled bittersweetly. "I have to go." She leaned close and kissed me. I wrapped my arms around her and felt her hot tears against my cheek. "You're my fallen angel. Don't lose your humanity over this. It isn't worth it. He's done enough. Taken enough. Don't let him suck you into the vortex too." She stepped back.

"Scott's dead, Jade. He can't hurt you anymore."

"Not me." She slung her carry-on over her shoulder.

"You're waging a war you can't win."

"I know what I'm doing."

"That's what worries me." She took a few steps toward the gate. "I'll call you when I land and let you know I'm safe."

I smiled. "You better."

FOR MORE LUCIEN CROSS, READ *ON TILT* (ALEXIS PARKER #14).

CHECK OUT MY OTHER SERIES BY VISITING:

http://www.alexisparkerseries.com

SIGN-UP TO BE NOTIFIED ABOUT THE LATEST RELEASES.

http://www.alexisparkerseries.com/newsletter

ABOUT THE AUTHOR

G.K. Parks is the author of the Alexis Parker series. The first novel, *Likely Suspects,* tells the story of Alexis' first foray into the private sector.

G.K. Parks received a Bachelor of Arts in Political Science and History. After spending some time in law school, G.K. changed paths and earned a Master of Arts in Criminology/Criminal Justice. Now all that education is being put to use creating a fictional world based upon years of study and research.

You can find additional information on G.K. Parks and the Alexis Parker series by visiting our website at
www.alexisparkerseries.com

Made in the USA
Monee, IL
29 January 2024

52610517R00080